总 主 编　张慧媛
副总主编　林立棻
顾　　问　[美] Xiaodan Huang
　　　　　[美] Yini Hu

创 新 思 维

英语综合教程

（第三册）

主　编　赵　培　王雪梅

副主编　袁俊娥　王成霞　邢桂丽

编　委　孙丰田　徐亮璎或　赵燕婷

中国人民大学出版社
·北京·

我国的大学英语教育自从上个世纪的教学改革开始至今已经取得了长足的进步，但在大学英语教学下的高职高专英语的改革却比较匮乏。随着近几年对高职高专英语的重视，各高职院校都对英语教学进行了改革。而本书的编纂者都是多年从事高职高专英语教育教学研究的一线教师，深知高职高专学生所需，也因此更能体会到高职高专英语教学改革的迫切性。

我们改革英语教材的目的是：（1）培养学生的创造性思维能力；（2）促进学生的职业能力的提升；（3）巧妙地兼顾对学生参加英语应用能力考试的训练；（4）培养学生独立思考、自主学习的能力；（5）提高学生的学习积极性。同时激发教师的教学兴趣，促进教师向"以学生为中心"教学理念的转变和教学质量的提高。

英语教学的最终目的是希望学生能把所学运用到实际生活和工作中，而如何把有用的知识传授给学生，则是本套教材所着重强调的部分。该套教材具备以下特色：

1. 吸取传统教材中的精华，改变传统教材的刻板。通过听说读写练的改革来使整套教材充满知识性、实用性以及趣味性。

2. 在课文选择方面，考虑到高职高专学生的特色，选择了具有文化意义又贴近现实生活的短文。通过知识点的扩展，学生不仅可以了解到英语国家的文化特色，更可以学习到地道、实用的英语表达方式。在针对课文的练习中，除了保留一部分针对考级的练习题外，还大量增加了提高学生主动性的图片练习以及能够发挥学生创造力的练习。

3. 听力方面则是以课文主题为背景提供相关的电影片段，使学生能够通过电影这一娱乐手段学习到更多、更实用的英语。听力原文除了以电影为媒介外，还增添了地道英语的听力练习。通过两者综合的讲练，使学生能够对所学的知识产生兴趣并且能够运用到实际生活中去。

4. 在说的方面，仍以电影片段为蓝本，让学生来判断并整理出在不同场合的正确表达方式以及需要注意的文化差异。整理后，学生可以根据自己的实际并发挥创新能力把电影中的语言运用到真正的学习生活中。

5. 在写作方面，呈现以课文主题为背景的写作练习，通过词汇、短语、句型以及格式等全方位的辅导，使学生能够有效、快速地掌握英文写作技巧，从而打破学生英文写作的障碍。

本套教程把听说读写紧密联系在一起，通过创新性的思维练习，让学生能够主动学习，并且在学习中发挥创造力和想象力，把寓教于乐真正地融合到一起，使学生真正体验到学习英语的乐趣所在。

《创新思维英语综合教程》由北京、新疆、山东、江西等省、市、自治区的教师共同编写完成。张洪颖、金继荣主编第一册；廖莎莎、董晓霞主编第二册；赵培和王雪梅主编第三册。

我们特别聘请来自美国的教育专家肖尼州立大学的终身教授 Xiaodan Huang 博士和 Yini Hu 女士为顾问并对本套教程进行审订。我们对她们严谨细致、一丝不苟的工作，特别是对每个单元语言表达的斟酌表示衷心感谢。

本套教程得到了教育部高职高专英语类专业教学指导委员会秘书长牛健教授的大力支持和指导，在此表示衷心感谢。

特别感谢中国人民大学出版社，他们高效务实的工作作风和严谨的工作态度使本套教程保质保量与广大读者见面。

本套教程引用了个别材料，由于种种原因未能找到原作者，请原作者看到后立即与我们联系，特地在此一并表示衷心感谢。

本套教程的编写是理念上一种新的尝试，请专家和同行批评指正。

编　者

2010 年 10 月 15 日

第三册内容简介

　　本册教材共 6 个单元，每个单元的听、说、读、写、练模块延续了第一、二册的设计特点——运用创造性思维，并与学生应用能力实践、创造性思维能力训练、学生职业能力培养融为一体。教材根据高职高专学生已有的第一、二册英语学习基础的特点，选择反映西方人现实生活的 300 词以上的语言材料进行改编，如有学生喜欢的宇宙探索、美国流行音乐、体育（足球）、3D 电影，还有与学生专业有关的网络、创新性司法等，并且保持了每一篇课文的创造性思维设计风格，以便增加课堂的趣味性，提高教师的教学兴趣。

　　本册听、说模块主要突出训练学生在情景模拟中说英语，模式仍然是按照"句型—学习—听—说—练习"进行设计，向学生呈现地道的、实用的英语表达方式，并运用了如英语电影片段、广告、录像、场景、图片等多种手段来训练学生的听说和创造性思维。

　　写与练模块的设计仍然紧扣课文，并结合全国英语应用能力三级考试的题型设计进行，使学生的学习既不脱离课文又解除了他们对英语应用能力三级考试的担忧，也解决了以往高职英语教材与英语应用能力三级考试脱节的问题。练习模块还增加了训练学生创新思维、发挥学生创造力和培养学生自主学习的创新综合作业，以促进学生英语学习和职业能力的提高。

Contents

Space Exploration

 Listening

Dialogue One   Oceans on Mars

Words and Expressions (I)

bury	/'beri/	vt.	埋葬；隐藏
change one's mind			改变主意
cross-bedding		n.	交错层
cruise	/kruːz/	n.	乘船游览
definite	/'definit/	adj.	确切的
deposit	/di'pɔzit/	n.	沉淀物
detect	/di'tekt/	vt.	发现；察觉；探测
element	/'elimənt/	n.	元素
look like			看起来像
measure	/'meʒə/	vt.	测量
mineral	/'minərəl/	n.	矿物 adj. 矿物的
not…any longer			不再
potassium	/pə'tæsjəm/	n.	钾
proof	/pruːf/	n.	证据；证明
shoreline		n.	海岸线
spectrometer	/spek'trɔmitə/	n.	分光仪；分光计
sulfate	/'sʌlfeit/	n.	硫酸盐
ten times the size of			是……的十倍
the amount of			数量
thorium	/'θɔːriəm/	n.	钍
water ripple			静水涟漪

Patterns（I）

Learn the following sentence patterns to practice listening and speaking.

1. —**Have you heard** two new oceans were discovered?
   —Where?
2. —**I thought** scientists weren't sure if Mars had oceans or not.
   —They weren't.
3. **What has changed their minds?**
4. —**What did they find?**
   —**They found** the shorelines of a younger ocean about
   ten times the size of the Mediterranean Sea, and an
   older ocean **twice that size**.
5. **It's too bad** those oceans still aren't there.
6. There wasn't definite proof.

 Exercise（I）

This section is to test your ability to understand Dialogue One. There are five questions for Dialogue One. After the dialogue, you should decide on the correct answer from the four choices marked A, B, C and D given below.

1. How many new oceans have been discovered on Mars according to Dialogue One?

   A. One.　　　　B. Two.　　　　C. Three.　　　　D. Four.

2. Which of the following is NOT evidence of ocean on Mars?

   A. Sulfates and other salts.　　　　B. Cross-bedding.

   C. Tiny mineral deposits.　　　　D. Gamma Ray.

3. What has made scientists believe that Mars had oceans?

   A. Things discovered by the Mars Opportunity Rover.

   B. Appearance of the northern lowlands of Mars.

   C. Gamma Ray evidence.

   D. Not mentioned in the dialogue.

4. The gamma-ray spectrometer on the Mars Odyssey spacecraft can measure all the following EXCEPT _____.

    A. potassium   B. thorium   C. steel   D. iron

5. How long are the shorelines of the younger ocean?

    A. Ten times the size of the Mediterranean Sea.

    B. Nine times the size of the Mediterranean Sea.

    C. Twice the size of the Mediterranean Sea.

    D. Twenty times the size of the Mediterranean Sea.

Dialogue Two   Farewell Sun

Words and Expressions (II)

be bad for			对……有害
black dwarf	/dwɔːf/		黑矮星
burn out			烧光，熄灭
contract	/kən'trækt/	*vi.*	订约；收缩
crisp	/krisp/	*n.*	油炸马铃薯片
energy	/'enədʒi/	*n.*	能量
hold on			等一等
hydrogen	/'haidrədʒən/	*n.*	氢
nuclear reactor			核反应堆
radius	/'reidiəs/	*n.*	半径
run out			用完，耗尽
what is called			所谓的
Who knows?			谁知道呢？

Patterns (II)

Learn the following sentence patterns to practice listening and speaking.

1. —**You mean** one day the sun will disappear?

    —Not exactly disappear, but the sun will eventually burn out and die.

2. —**Hold on.** Start from the beginning.

   —OK.

3. —Like any reactor, the sun needs fuel to keep going.

   —But then the fuel will **run out**.

4. The sun will then become **what's called** a red giant, and its radius will reach just past the orbit of Venus.

5. **Who knows?** By then humans might be living on another planet.

 Exercise (Ⅱ)

Listen to Dialogue Two and complete it with what you hear.

Don: Wow, what a beautiful sunset.

Yael: Enjoy it while it lasts. The sun won't be around forever, you know.

Don: You mean one day the sun will disappear?

Yael: Not exactly disappear, but the sun will eventually burn out and die.

Don: Whoa, hold on. Start from the beginning.

Yael: OK. Like all stars the sun is basically a giant nuclear reactor that burns hydrogen to _____1_____ energy. But like any reactor, the sun needs fuel to keep going. It's been going strong for around 4.5 billion years, and will probably keep burning for about _____2_____.

Don: But then the fuel will run out.

Yael: Exactly. And when it does, gravity will cause the sun's core to contract. When it contracts the core will get hotter, which will heat up the sun's _____3_____ and make them expand. The sun will then become what's called a red giant, and its radius will reach just past the orbit of Venus.

Don: Which is _____4_____.

Yael: We'll be burned to a crisp.

Don: That sounds painful.

Yael: After a few billion years the core will eventually _____5_____ to become a black dwarf.

Don: So we're pretty much doomed.

Yael: Yes, but not for billions of years. Who knows? By then humans might be living on another planet.

Don: I think someone's been watching too much cable TV.

 Exercise (Ⅲ)

Creative Thinking

Enjoy a part of the film *The Chronicles of Narnia* and discuss its result. You are required to act it.

 Speaking

① Work in pairs: Make a dialogue.

Please choose one of the following pictures, and then according to the sentence patterns you have just learnt, make up a dialogue with your partner. You are encouraged to use your rich imagination.

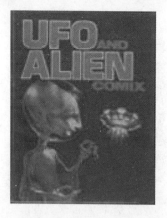

Vocabulary ▼

Alien/E.T.(the Extra-Terrestrial)	外星人
astronaut/taikonaut	宇航员，太空人
LM(Lunar Module)	登月舱
manned spacecraft engineering	载人航天事业
UFO(Unidentified Flying Object)	飞碟，不明飞行物

Questions

1. **What do you think of** the movie *AVATAR*?

2. **What if** you encountered an alien from outer space?

Ⅱ Watch the videos and answer the following questions.

Vocabulary ▼

adopt /ə'dɔpt/	*vt.*	收养；采取；接受
barrier /'bæriə/	*n.*	障碍；栅栏；篱笆墙
be committed to…		致力于……，忠于……
be supposed to do…		应该……，被期望做……
curiosity /ˌkjuri'ɔsiti/	*n.*	好奇，好奇心
go against…		反对/抗……
horizon /hə'raizən/	*n.*	地平线；视野；眼界
indigenous population		土著居民
invest in…		投资于……
make a difference		有影响，很重要
on the brink of…		濒临……
step by step		逐步地

Video 1

Let's embrace space!

Video 2

Video 3

Task 1 Watch Video 1 and identify the steps of space exploration.

	What is this step about?	What has been done or needs to be done?
Step 1		
Step 2		
Step 3		
Step 4		

Task 2 Watch Video 2 and identify the US new space strategy.

_____

Task 3 Watch Video 3 and tell how you would deal with the aliens if you were in the same situation as in the movie *AVATAR*.

_____

Ⅲ Work in groups.

Some people argue that putting money and energy in space exploration is a great waste. It is better if they are used to solve current problems. What's your opinion? Discuss with your partners, and choose a representative to report to the whole class.

Where there is a will, there is a way.

Text

Teacher in Space Answer Questions from Students

Morgan (left) and McAuliffe in 1986 [NASA]

Barbara Morgan

Barbara Morgan was a teacher-turned-astronaut, speaking from more than three hundred twenty kilometers above the Earth. she was greeting students of the northwestern state of Idaho. They gathered at the Discovery Center in Boise on Tuesday to ask the astronauts questions by video link.

CHILDREN: "Hello from Idaho!"

The astronauts already knew what the questions would be. One student asked what stars looked like from space.

The answer was that the space shuttle and the space station are kept brightly lit, so it is difficult to see a lot of stars.

BARBARA MORGAN: "In fact, one way to think about that when we're on the International Space Station and all the lights are on when we look outside, it's very much like trying to look at the stars when you're in Boise. You can see some, but then if you go up high in the mountains, up to McCall, and you have all the lights out."

Barbara Morgan taught in an elementary school in McCall, Idaho for many years before she was trained to become an astronaut at age 55. She and six other astronauts arrived Friday on the shuttle Endeavour to bring supplies and new equipment to the international station.

QUESTION: "Hi, I'm Sarah Blum. How does being a teacher relate with being an astronaut on this mission?"

BARBARA MORGAN: "Well, astronauts and teachers actually do the same things. We explore, we discover and we share. And the great thing about being a teacher is you get to do that with students. And the great thing about being an astronaut is you get to do it in space. And those are absolutely wonderful jobs."

Barbara Morgan first prepared for a shuttle flight more than twenty years ago. She trained in case NASA needed a substitute for Christa McAuliffe, the first teacher in space.

Then, in 1986, Christa McAuliffe died with the Challenger crew when the shuttle exploded shortly after launch.

After the disaster, NASA officials *barred* other civilians from shuttle flights. But in 1998, they created a new position for teachers to become fully trained astronauts. Barbara Morgan is NASA's first "educator astronaut" launched into orbit.

(373 words)

New Words

astronaut	/'æstrənɔːt/	*n.* 宇航员
bar	/bɑː/	*n.* 酒吧；障碍　*vt.* ban 禁止
basically	/'beisikəli/	*adv.* mainly 主要地，基本上
crew	/kruː/	*n.* 队，组；全体人员，全体船员
disaster	/ˌdi'zɑːstə/	*n.* 灾难，灾祸；不幸
Endeavour	/in'devə/	"奋进"号航天飞机
equipment	/i'kwipmənt/	*n.* device 设备，装备；器材

explode	/ik'spləud/	v. 爆炸
launch	/lɔ:ntʃ, lɑ:ntʃ/	vt. & n. 发射（导弹、火箭等）；发起
link	/liŋk/	n. 链环，环节；联系，关系
mission	/'miʃən/	n. task 使命，任务；delegation 代表团
orbit	/'ɔ:bit/	n. 轨道；眼眶
supply	/sə'plai/	n. 物资；供应品；贮备量
substitute	/'sʌbstitju:t, -tu:t/	n. 代替者，替代品　v. 用……代替，代替
video	/'vidiəu/	n. 视频　adj. 视频的；录像的；电视的

Phrases & Expressions

get to	到达；开始；着手处理；接触到
in case	万一；假使
relate with	使相关，使符合
space shuttle	航天飞机
space station	空间站，太空站

Proper Nouns

Boise	/'bɔisi/	博伊西（美国爱达荷州首府）
Idaho	/'aidəhəu/	美国爱达荷州
McCall		麦考尔（美国爱达荷州的一个城市）
NASA	/'næsə, 'nei-/	abbr. 美国国家航空航天局 (National Aeronautics and Space Administration)

Focus on

bar　launch　basically　supplies　explore　link　relate　discover
crew　get to　in case　equipment　substitute

Study Independently

You are required to study independently the words and sentences given. Discuss what you have learned and think over the usages in the text.

bar

1. The wet **bar** of soap slid from my hands.
2. There are several **bars** in the hotel.
3. His bad English is a **bar** to his using new computer software.
4. Be sure to **bar** all the doors before you leave.
5. The police **barred** the exits in an attempt to prevent the terrorist's escape.

explore

1. Russia also plans new efforts to **explore** Mars.
2. Can you **explore** the market possibility for us?.
3. Our purpose is to **explore** the possibilities of developing trade with you.
4. I admire those explorers who ventured forth to **explore** new lands.

relate

1. All these questions **relate** to philosophy.
2. Happiness does not always **relate** to wealth.
3. The professor told his students to **relate** theory with practice.
4. We must **relate** the results with the cause.

link

1. The Great Lakes **link** the USA and Canada.
2. They planned to build a highway to **link** the two towns.
3. The new firm **linked** up with several big ones.
4. Doctors have found a definite **link** between smoking and lung cancer.

substitute

1. We shall soon **substitute** gas for coal.
2. Daydreaming cannot **substitute** for hard work.

3. Can you **substitute** for me at the meeting?

4. The manager was unable to attend but sent his deputy as a **substitute.**

5. They are studying to develop a **substitute** for this kind of medicine.

 Practicing & Developing

Comprehension

I **Choose the best answer to each of the following questions.**

1. Where was Barbara Morgan speaking to the students?

   A. In the northwestern state of Idaho.

   B. At the Discovery Center in Boise.

   C. On the shuttle Endeavour.

   D. On the International Space Station.

2. Why is it difficult to see a lot of stars on the space station?

   A. All the lights are on.　　　B. All the lights are out.

   C. They are far from the stars.　　D. There are not many stars.

3. What does the word "bar" in the first line of the last paragraph mean?

   A. Agree.　　B. Permit.　　C. Support.　　D. Forbid.

4. Which of the following statements is true according to the passage?

   A. Barbara Morgan is America's first woman astronaut.

   B. Barbara Morgan became an astronaut at the age of 55.

   C. Barbara Morgan had trained as McAuliffe's backup for shuttle flight.

   D. NASA recruited more teachers to fly in space soon after the Challenger disaster.

5. What mission did Morgan carry out on the shuttle Endeavour?

   A. To answer questions from the students.

   B. To bring supplies and equipment to the space station.

   C. To bring equipment and materials back to Earth.

   D. To train for the space shuttle flight.

Vocabulary and Structure

II **Make the best choice to fill in each blank.**

1. The _____ of space shuttle Atlantis is being delayed until Monday.

    A. crew   B. astronaut   C. orbit   D. launch

2. Only a dozen countries still _____ people with HIV from entering their own countries.

    A. launch   B. bar   C. explore   D. relate

3. He has collected many proverbs and popular sayings that _____ to weather.

    A. relate   B. turn   C. benefit   D. combine

4. There is an obvious _____ between unemployment and the crime rate.

    A. crew   B. launch   C. link   D. substitute

5. When a member of a team is injured, a _____ plays in his/her place.

    A. launch   B. link   C. crew   D. substitute

6. Farmers love the fall season because they _____ harvest and sell the results of their hard work.

    A. get to   B. set out   C. come to   D. go over

7. _____ anything important happens, please call me up.

    A. Even if   B. In case   C. As if   D. Even when

8. _____, it is energy that makes the world go round.

    A. Basically   B. Specially   C. Occasionally   D. Unfortunately

9. A store sells foods and various household _____.

    A. mission   B. crew   C. supplies   D. substitute

10. One helicopter crashed into a mountain with three _____ members on board.

    A. shuttle   B. disaster   C. astronaut   D. crew

III **Fill in each blank with the right form of the word given in the bracket.**

1. China is the third country after Russia and the United States _____ (launch) a man into space.

2. With this _____ (equip), you can explore a new world of adventure and underwater beauty!

3. We would like to establish business _____ (relate) with you to expand Russian market.

4. The research of deficiency diseases led to his _____ (discover) of vitamins, which he named in 1912.

5. The new _____ (explore) plan would allow four astronauts to stay on the moon for a week—twice as long as the Apollo-mission astronauts were allowed.

6. There is a crying need for more medical _____ (supply) for the refugees.

7. Found to have taken drugs, Ben Johnson was _____ (bar) from international athletics for two years.

8. Each soccer team has eleven players and three _____ (substitute), or reserve players.

9. The Belgian language is closely _____ (relate) to French.

10. If you go on making so much noise, I shall have no choice but _____ (complain) to the police.

IV **Find the items equivalent to those given in Chinese in the table below.**

A. military supplies	B. medical supplies
C. electronic equipment	D. launch window
E. heating equipment	F. shuttle diplomacy
G. launch vehicle	H. office supplies
I. first aid supplies	J. launch an attack
K. space shuttle	L. household supplies
M. launch a rocket	N. printing equipment
O. relief supplies	P. medical equipment
Q. launch a satellite	R. market supplies
S. air-conditioning equipment	T. launch a debate
U. shuttle race	V. shuttle bus
W. launch pad	X. launch site

Example: (K) 航天飞机　(W) 发射台

1. (　) 运载火箭	(　) 穿梭外交
2. (　) 急救用品	(　) 救灾物资
3. (　) 发射火箭	(　) 展开论战
4. (　) 军用物资	(　) 医疗设备
5. (　) 空调设备	(　) 日常用品

 Choose the best translation.

1. On the other hand, there are plenty of programs designed for anyone who simply wants to explore their interest in a particular subject.

   A. 另一方面，有许多程序是为那些对探究某一领域感兴趣的人设计的。

   B. 另一方面，有许多课程是为那些想发掘自己对某一学科的兴趣的人开设的。

   C. 另一方面，有许多节目是由那些对某一特定的主题感兴趣的人设计的。

   D. 另一方面，有许多方案是由那些想探索某一特定领域的人设计的。

2. I believe that teaching is successful only when students are able to relate what they learn to real life.

   A. 我认为，只有当让学生能够把所学的知识与现实生活联系起来时，教学才是成功的。

   B. 我认为，只有当学生能够把所学的知识应用到现实生活中时，教学才是成功的。

   C. 我认为，只有当学生能够在现实生活中学到知识，教学才是成功的。

   D. 我认为，只有当学生能够在实践中掌握学到的知识，教学才是成功的。

3. The results show that the system has basically met the design objectives.

   A. 结果表明，设计的系统总体上符合了预期的设计标准。

   B. 结果表明，设计的系统基本上满足了预期的设计目标。

   C. 结果表明，设计的系统达到了设计的基本要求。

   D. 结果表明，系统设计满足了预期的基本的设计目标。

4. What matters is not whether you work independently or with a crew but whether you have independent ideas and thoughts.

   A. 无论你是否独立工作还是与团队合作，你都要有独立的想法和思想。

   B. 重要的不是你是否有独立的想法和思想，而是你能否独立地或者和团队工作。

C. 重要的不是你是否独立地工作还是和团队工作，而是你是否有独立的想法和思想。

D. 重要的不仅是你能否独立地或与他人合作，你还要有独立的想法和思想。

5. Our mission is to offer the absolute best service and selection on medical equipment and supplies at the best possible price.

A. 我们的宗旨是以最优惠的价格，提供绝对一流的服务和医疗设备及用品。

B. 我们的愿望是能够得到绝对一流的服务，选择到物美价廉的医疗设备及用品。

C. 我们的使命是以最优惠的价格提供绝对一流的服务和医疗设备及用品。

D. 我们的目的是提供绝对一流的服务和价格合理的医疗设备及用品供您选择。

Assignment

1. 适合所有专业

Topic: **Anticipate the Future Earth**

Grading Criteria:

1. Creativity (20%)

2. Language usage (30%)

3. Using PPT (30%)

4. Using the words which you have learnt in Unit One (20%)

Sample 见《高职高专英语创造性思维训练集》，北京：中国人民大学出版社，2010：p89

2. 适合广告专业

Topic: **Advertisement of Space Journey**

As a designer, please make an advertisement for space journey, show your ideas and explain them.

Standards of grading:

    1. Creativity (20%)

    2. Correct language (30%)

    3. Using PPT (30%)

    4. Using the words which you have learnt in Unit One (20%)

Sample 见《高职高专英语创造性思维训练集》，北京：中国人民大学出版社，
    2010：p91

3. 适合旅游专业

Topic: **Introduction to Space Journey**

    As a tour guide, please introduce a space journey to your tourists.

Grading Criteria:

    1. Creativity (20%)

    2. Language usage (30%)

    3. Using PPT (30%)

    4. Using the words which you have learnt in Unit One (20%)

Sample 见《高职高专英语创造性思维训练集》，北京：中国人民大学出版社，
    2010：p94

Reading

Space Exploration

Apollo Twelve lifted off only four months after the Apollo Eleven flight. Rain had fallen the night before. The clouds cleared, but more rain was expected. Space officials decided the weather was safe enough for them to launch the spacecraft.

Thirty-six seconds after lift-off, lightning hit the huge Saturn Five rocket. The Apollo spacecraft lost electrical power to its control system. The astronauts worked calmly to get the power back on. Then lightning struck again. And power was lost again.

The lightning, however, did not affect the Saturn rocket. The rocket continued to push the spacecraft on its path. The astronauts soon fixed the electrical problem. The situation returned to normal. Apollo Twelve could continue its flight to the moon.

All three astronauts of Apollo Twelve were Navy fliers. Charles Conrad was the flight commander. Richard Gordon was pilot of the command module. Alan Bean was pilot of the moon lander.

After four days, Apollo Twelve was near its landing area on the moon. It would land in an area called the Ocean of Storms. The Ocean of Storms was about two thousand kilometers west of the place where Apollo Eleven had landed.

Richard Gordon remained in the command module circling the moon. Charles Conrad and Alan Bean flew the lander craft to the surface. They came down near Surveyor Three, an unmanned spacecraft that had landed on the moon two years before. Surveyor had sent back six thousand pictures of the moon before it stopped working.

Conrad stepped out of the lander onto the moon. He described the surface as he walked away from the spacecraft. "Oh," he said, "is this soft! I don't sink in it too far."

Alan Bean followed Charles Conrad to the surface. The two astronauts collected about thirty-five kilograms of rocks. They left five scientific instruments designed to send information back to Earth. And they visited the old Surveyor spacecraft.

The two astronauts spent more than thirty-one hours on the moon. Then they returned to the orbiting command module and started back to Earth. They landed in the Pacific Ocean, only six kilometers from the ship that waited to rescue them.

(358 words)

New Words

affect	/əˈfekt/	vt. 影响
calmly	/ˈkɑːmli/	adv. 冷静地；平静地；安静地
circle	/ˈsəːkl/	vt. 环绕……移动
commander	/kəˈmɑːndə/	n. 指挥官
fix	/fiks/	vt. 使固定；修理；安装
flier	/ˈflaiə/	n. 飞行员；飞行物
lander	/ˈlændə/	n. 着陆器
lightning	/ˈlaitniŋ/	n. 闪电
navy	/ˈneivi/	n. 海军
orbit	/ˈɔːbit/	v. 绕轨道运行，旋转运动，转圈
path	/pɑːθ, pæθ/	n. 小路；轨道
pilot	/ˈpailət/	n. 飞行员；领航员
rescue	/ˈreskjuː/	vt. 援救，救出，营救

| scientific | /saiən'tifik/ | *adj.* 科学的 |
| spacecraft | /'speiskrɑ:ft, -kræft/ | *n.* 宇宙飞船，航天器 |

Phrases & Expressions

command module	指挥舱；驾驶舱
lift off	（火箭等）发射；（直升机）起飞
remain in	待在屋里，不外出；保持处于（某种状态）
scientific instrument	科学仪器
unmanned spacecraft	无人驾驶飞机；无人宇宙飞船

 **Exercises**

Reading Comprehension

Choose the best answer to each of the following questions.

1. What was the weather like before the spacecraft was launched?

   A. It was raining.   B. It was cloudy.   C. It was sunny.   D. It was clear.

2. What happened to the spacecraft after lift-off?

   A. Lighting struck the spacecraft.

   B. The electrical power was lost.

   C. The control system broke down.

   D. The lighting strikes damaged the Saturn rocket.

3. Which of the following is true according to the passage?

   A. Surveyor Three was still working properly.

   B. All the astronauts walked on the moon.

   C. The surface of the moon was soft.

   D. The spacecraft did not land on Earth safely.

4. What did the astronauts do on the moon?

   A. They performed engineering tests.

   B. They collected a large amount of rocks.

C. They repaired some scientific instruments.

D. They sent information back to Earth.

5. How long did the space flight take?

A. About 10 days.   B. About 8 days.   C. About a week.   D. Half a month.

Grammar

动词不定式(the Infinitive)

Pretest

Choose the best answer to each of the following questions.

1. He hurried to the station, _____ he forgot to take his ticket.

A. to find   B. only to find   C. found   D. only finding

2. _____ time and labor, we have to cut down the number of workforce.

A. Saved   B. To save   C. Saving   D. Save

3. Tom could do nothing but _____ to his mother that he lied.

A. admit   B. admits   C. admitting   D. to admit

4. A doctor can expect _____ at any time of the day.

A. calling   B. to call   C. to be called   D. being called

5. The idea is difficult _____ in English.

A. to express it   B. to express   C. express it   D. to be expressed

6. She made a candle _____ us light.

A. give   B. gave   C. to give   D. given

7. At the shopping-centre, she didn't know what _____ and _____ sadly.

A. to buy; leave   B. to be bought; left

C. to buy; left   D. was to buy; leave

8. Is the house comfortable for us _____?

A. to live   B. to be living   C. living   D. to live in

不定式的基本形式由"to+ 动词原形"构成，其否定形式是 not to do。不定式不失动词的特点，可以带自己的宾语或状语，构成不定式短语。它没有人称和数的变化，但有时态和语态的变化。不定式在句中除了不做谓语外，可做主语、表语、宾语、定语、状语、补足语。

一、不定式的作用

1. 做主语

不定式做主语，一般表示具体的某次动作。如：

To take the position means taking responsibility. 承担那个职位就意味着承担责任。

不定式做主语置于句首时，常用先行词 **it** 做形式主语，而将真实主语不定式移置后边，即用句型 "**It +be+ adj./n.+ to v.**"，如：

It is interesting to learn English. 学习英语很有趣。

2. 做表语

不定式做表语常表示将来的动作，如：

The most important thing we should do is to solve the problem.

我们应该做的最重要的事情就是解决这个问题。

3. 做宾语

（1）做动词的宾语

下列及物动词后，常跟不定式做宾语：afford, agree, ask, attempt, beg, choose, decide, demand, desire, expect, fail, fear, help, intend, learn, love, manage, offer, plan, prepare, want, need, hope, wish, know, pretend, refuse 等。如：

He managed to overcome the difficulty. 他设法克服了困难。

如做宾语的不定式后有补足语时，用先行词 **it** 做形式宾语，而将真实宾语不定式移至宾语补足语之后，即用 "主语 + 谓语 + **it** + 宾补 + **to do**" 句型，如：

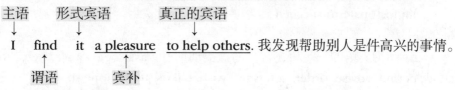

I find it a pleasure to help others. 我发现帮助别人是件高兴的事情。

（2）做介词的宾语

介词 but 可用不定式做宾语，如：

The children had no choice but to accept the arrangement. 孩子们没有选择，只得接受安排。

在谓语动词中含有 do 的各种形式时，but 后接不定式，要省略不定式符号 to，如：

She had nothing to do but stay at home. 她无事可做，只能待在家里。

4. 做定语

不定式做定语都应放在它所修饰的名词或代词后面。

（1）only, last, next, 序数词或形容词最高级修饰的名词常用不定式做定语，如：

He is always the first one to come and the last one to leave. 他总是第一个到，最后一个走。

（2）不定式做定语如果与修饰的名词或代词有动宾关系，应注意不及物动词的不定式后要带介词，并且不定式后不能再带宾语，如：

I have something important to do. (do something: 及物动词 + 宾语)

Mother gives me a piece of paper to write on.

(write on the paper: 不及物动词 + 介词 + 宾语)

5. 做状语

（1）做目的状语

I got up early in order to catch the first bus. 为了赶第一班车，我起得很早。

so as to 不能置于句首，in order to 可以。

（2）做结果状语

He was so angry as not to be able to speak. 他气得说不出话来。

不定式前面和 only 连用表示没有意想到的结果，如：

He hurried to the station, only to find the train had left. 他匆忙赶向车站，却发现火车早已开走。

（3）在某些形容词如 sorry, glad, happy 等后面做状语。

I am fortunate to succeed.

6. 做补足语

（1）动词宾语的补足语，常见的这类动词有：ask, beg, cause, help, force, allow, permit, advise, order, get, want, wish, tell 等（没有 hope sb. to do, suggest sb. to do 和 agree sb. to do 的形式）。如：

He asked me to do him a favor. 他请我帮忙。

（2）感官动词如 see, look at, watch, hear, listen to, feel, notice 等，以及使役动词如 make, have, let 后的宾语补足语要用动词原形，不能带 to; help 之后可

省略 to, 也可不省略 to，如：

I saw the teacher enter the classroom. 我看见老师走进了教室。

但在被动语态中，不定式一律带 to。

Everybody, old or young, is expected to obey the law. 任何人，不论长幼，都应该遵守法律。

在谓语动词 think, consider, suppose, believe, imagine, prove, find 等后面跟 to be 做宾补，不跟 to do。如：

I found him (to be) an honest boy. 我发现他是一个诚实的孩子。

7. 疑问词 + 不定式（短语）

这一结构可做主语、宾语、表语。如：

I don't know whether to stay or leave. （做宾语）我不知道是去还是留。

When to carry out the plan has not been decided yet. （做主语）何时执行这个计划还没有决定。

The problem is how to rescue the homeless people. （做表语）问题是如何解救这些无家可归的人们。

二、动词不定式的时态变化形式（以 do 为例）

时态＼语态	主动态	被动态
一般式	to do	to be done
完成式	to have done	to have been done
进行式	to be doing	
完成进行式	to have been doing	

1. 不定式的时态（需首先根据上面的要点尤其是划线部分的内容来确定是否使用动词不定式，然后再考虑使用下面某个时态。）

(1) 一般式：**to + do**

当不定式所表达的动作在谓语动词之后发生时，用不定式一般式，如：

I **hope** to see you soon. 我希望很快见到你。

(2) 进行式：**to be + doing**

当不定式所表达的动作与谓语动词同时发生，并强调动作正在进行的情景，或持续性时，不定式用进行式，如：

He **pretended** to be sleeping when I came back. 我回来时他假装在睡觉。

(3) 完成式：**to have done**

如果不定式的动作发生在谓语动词之前，不定式要用完成式，如：

I am sorry to have put you to so much trouble. 我很抱歉给你带来那么多麻烦。

(4) 完成进行式：**to have been doing**

如果强调不定式所表示的动作从过去某一时刻起一直持续到某一时刻，不定式用完成进行式，强调动作的持续性，不强调结果。如：

Mary **seems** to have been studying for three hours. 玛丽似乎学了三个小时了。

2. 不定式的语态

当不定式的逻辑主语与不定式是被动关系时，不定式一般用被动式。如：

This is the work to be done. 这是要做的工作。

Practice

Identify **the infinitive** in the text. (The reference key can be found in this unit.)

Practical Writing and Reading

Agenda

议程表以直观的方式表示计划的活动或预约，一般由标题和内容两部分组成。

标题通常包括：单位名称、地点、日期、开始和结束时间。内容包括：具体项目、主持人、时间分配等。

Sample:

Professional Exchange: Educators from China and NOVA
March 21, 2010   9:30a.m.-12:30p.m.
Room 211   Howsmon Building
Northern Virginia Community College

Time	Topic	Presenter
9:15a.m.-9:30a.m.	Refreshments	
9:30a.m.-9:50a.m.	Welcome and Introductions	Ms. Heidi Adamson Director, Academy for Culture and Language
9:50a.m.-10:10a.m.	About NOVA	Dr. Dariel Martin Dean, Division of Science and Technologies
10:10a.m.-10:30a.m.	Culture and Communication	Dr. Charles Korn Dean, Division of Communication Studies
10:30a.m.-10:40a.m.	Break	
10:40a.m.-11:00a.m.	Distance Learning	Mr. Robert Loser Faculty and Instructional Designer
11:00a.m.-11:20a.m.	NOVA StarTalk	Dr. Peter Cohen Faculty and Instructional Designer, ELI
11:20a.m.-11:40a.m.	Online Course Management	Ms. Alicia Tucker Faculty, Department of History
11:40a.m.-12:00p.m.	ESL for International Students	Mr. Bill Woodard Faculty and Director, ESL program
12:00p.m.-12:30p.m.	Discussion and Picture-Taking	

Task 1

根据下面题目要求，写一张议程表。

（1）主题：有关旅游发展

（2）时间：2010 年 7 月 25 日，地点：新华酒店 211 会议室

（3）内容：8:30-9:00 报到，地点：酒店大堂

9:00-9:30 会议开始，李华教授致开幕词

9:30-10:50 张明教授，题目：未来旅游

10:50-11:20 休息

11:20-13:00 午餐

13:00-15:30 分组讨论

15:30-16:00 休息

16:00-18:00 晚餐，李华教授致闭幕词

Task 2

Directions: The following is an *agenda*. After reading it, you are required to complete the outline below it (No. 1 through No. 5). You should write your answer briefly (in no more than 3 words).

CONFERENCE ON CUSTOMER SERVICE AGENDA

Monday, March 5

9:00 a.m.   Registration

2:30 p.m.   Confirm location of reception & dinner due to weather

6:00 p.m.   Preview Dinner to confirm set-up

7:00 p.m.   Welcome Reception & Dinner

10:00 p.m.   Conclusion of Evening

Tuesday, March 6

8:40 a.m.   Business Unit Strategy

10:25 a.m.   Break

10:40 a.m.　Digital Business Update

11:40 a.m.　Lunch (Boxed Lunch)

12:30 p.m.　Team-building Activities (Golf / Spa)

7:30 p.m.　Dinner

Wednesday, March 7

8:40 a.m.　Operations Update

11:00 a.m.　Break

11:10 a.m.　Business Units Focus Session Ⅰ: *Salon A, Salon B, Salon C*

12:40 p.m.　Business Units Focus Session Ⅱ & Working Lunch: *Salon A, Salon B*

2:10 p.m.　Business Units Focus Session Ⅲ: *Salon A C, 50 people; Salon B C, 50 people*

3:30 p.m.　Closing Remarks: *Salons D & E*

The agenda is about ABC Company _____1_____ conference.

The conference will last _____2_____days.

Time for digital business update: _____3_____

Activities for teambuilding on Tuesday: _____4_____

Places for Business Units Focus Session Ⅲ: _____5_____

The conference will end in closing remarks.

(Task 3)

Directions: The following is a ***meeting agenda***. After reading it, you should give brief answers to the 5 questions (No. 1 through No. 5). The answers (in no more than 3 words) should be written after the corresponding numbers.

MEETING AGENDA	
Project name:	System A Redesign Phase
Purpose, Objectives and Elements of the Meeting:	
Risk Identification Workshop	

Expected Attendees:		Date and Time:	9:00 am, November 1, 2010
M. Black (Chair) J. Clark A. Lim J. Turner S. Sutcliffe P. Green G. Hughson		Place:	Room 221, North Building

	Agenda Item	Person Responsible	Time
1	Introduction Review purpose of the workshop.	M. Black	5 mins
2	Risk Management Process Review the approach to risk management established for the SYSTEM A project.	M. Black	20 mins
3	Risk Identification Brainstorming Participate in a non-judgemental think-tank session to identify risks in each type and category and produce an initial list of risks.	All	100 mins

1. What project is the meeting about?

   The meeting is about _____ Redesign Phase.

2. How many people will attend the meeting?

   There are _____.

3. What will M. Black do during Risk Management Process?

   _____ to risk management established for the project.

4. Who will attend the Risk Identification Brainstorming?

   _____.

5. When will the meeting end?

   _____.

Translate the following passage.

　　Charles Conrad and Alan Bean flew the lander craft to the surface. They came down near Surveyor Three, an unmanned spacecraft that had landed on the moon two years before. Surveyor had sent back six thousand pictures of the moon before it stopped working.

_____

_____

_____

Key to the grammar practice:

1. They gathered at the Discovery Center in Boise on Tuesday *to ask* the astronauts questions by video link.

2. Basically the answer was that the space shuttle and the space station are kept brightly lit, so it is difficult *to see* a lot of stars.

3. In fact, one way *to think about* that when we're on the International Space Station and all the lights are on when we look outside, it's very much like trying *to look at* the stars when you're in Boise.

4. She and six other astronauts arrived Friday on the shuttle Endeavour *to bring* supplies and new equipment to the international station.

5. And the great thing about being a teacher is you get *to do* that with students. And the great thing about being an astronaut is you get *to do* it in space.

6. Barbara Morgan first prepared for a shuttle flight more than twenty years ago. She trained in case NASA needed a substitute for Christa McAuliffe, its choice *to become* the first teacher in space.

7. But in nineteen ninety-eight, they created a new position for teachers *to become* fully trained astronauts.

3-D Movies

Listening

Dialogue One   Seeing a Movie

Words and Expressions (I)

action comedy			动作喜剧
be based on			以……为基础
biographical	/baiˈɔgrəfikəl/	*adj.*	传记的
blockbuster	/ˈblɔkˌbʌstə/	*n.*	大片
chick flick			女性爱看的电影
depend on			取决于
have in mind			想到，考虑到
to be honest			说实话

Patterns (I)

Learn the following sentence patterns to practice listening and speaking.

1. —**Have you heard of** *Hot Fuzz*?

   —Yes. Isn't it directed by the same guy who directed *Shaun of the Dead*?

2. —**What do you think of the movie?**

   —**To be honest**, I didn't really like *Shaun of the Dead*.

3. —**Do you like** biographical/drama films?

—It **depends on** whom the film is about.

4. —**Which movie do you have in mind?**

—A new movie called *Becoming Jane* **based on** a true story about Jane Austen.

5. —**What time is it playing?**

—**It's on** at 8:00 pm at the Phoenix Theatre.

 Exercise (I)

This section is to test your ability to understand Dialogue One. There are five questions for Dialogue One. After the dialogue, you should decide on the correct answer from the four choices marked A, B, C and D given below.

1. Which two movies were directed by the same person?

A. *Hot Fuzz* and *Shaun of the Dead*.

B. *Hot Fuzz* and *You, Me and Dupree*.

C. *Shaun of the Dead* and *You, Me and Dupree*.

D. *You, Me and Dupree* and *Becoming Jane*.

2. What kind of film is *Becoming Jane*?

A. Action comedy.　　　　　　B. Biographical film.

C. Animated cartoon.　　　　　D. Science fiction.

3. Who played the leading roles in *You, Me and Dupree*?

A. Kate Hudson and Jane Austin.

B. Kate Hudson and Owen Wilson.

C. Jane Austin and Owen Wilson.

D. Not mentioned in the dialogue.

4. Which film did Jane and Neo decide to see at last?

A. *Hot Fuzz*.　　　　　　　B. *Shaun of the Dead*.

C. *You, Me and Dupree*.　　　D. *Becoming Jane*.

5. When did Jane and Neo meet at the theatre?

A. At 7:15 pm.　　B. At 7:30 pm.　　C. At 7:45 pm.　　D. At 8:00 pm.

Dialogue Two 4-D Movies

Words and Expressions (Ⅱ)

combine...with...			与……结合
Expo Park			世博园
have a look			看一看
pass through			通过
pavilion	/pə'viljən/	*n.*	临时展出馆
synchronization	/ˌsiŋkrənai'zeiʃən/	*n.*	同步
time-consuming	/'taimkənˌsuːmiŋ/	*adj.*	费时的
water spray			洒水，喷雾

Patterns (Ⅱ)

Learn the following sentence patterns to practice listening and speaking.

1. —What a long queue!

   —It's really timeconsuming to **pass through** the security checks.

2. —**How about** starting from the Saudi Arabia Pavilion?

   —Anything special?

3. —It's **one of** the most popular pavilions.

   —**Highlights of the pavilion include**: Garden with Chinese and Saudi Trees, Exotic Arabian Flavor, and The Treasure Cinema.

4. **That is**, 4-D movies are 3-D movies that have stuff you can feel.

5. In South Korea, the film *Avatar* **was presented as** a 4-D movie.

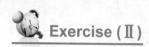

Exercise (Ⅱ)

Listen to Dialogue Two and complete it with what you hear.

Jack: What a long queue!

Lee: Yeah. It's really time-consuming to pass through the security checks.

Jack: Luckily I brought a small stool _____1_____.

Lee: So where shall we start after entering into the Expo Park? One day is obviously _____2_____ to have a good look.

Jack: How about starting from the Saudi Arabia Pavilion?

Lee: Anything special?

Jack: Yes, it's one of the most popular pavilions. Highlights of the pavilion include: Garden with Chinese and Saudi Trees, Exotic Arabian Flavor, and The Treasure Cinema. In the Treasure Cinema, visitors can experience 4-D movies, seeing many of the country's _____3_____ treasures.

Lee: 4-D movies? What's that? Can you be more specific?

Jack: Well, scientifically speaking, a 4-D movie is an entertainment presentation system combining a 3-D movie film with physical effects in the theatre, which occur in synchronization with the film. That is, 4-D movies are _____4_____ that have stuff you can feel. Some of the effects simulated in 4-D movies include rain, wind, strobe lights, and vibration. The use of water sprays and air jets is also common. In South Korea, the film *Avatar* was presented as a 4-D movie.

Lee: Incredible! You certainly know a lot about it.

Jack: I'm a big fan of movies.

Lee: Your words just aroused _____5_____. Let's start from Saudi Arabia Pavilion.

 Exercise (Ⅲ)

Creative Thinking

Enjoy a part of the film *Spiderman* and discuss its result. You are required to act it.

  Speaking

Ⅰ **Work in pairs: Make a dialogue.**

Please choose one of the following pictures, and then according to the sentence patterns you have just learnt, make up a dialogue with your partner. You are encouraged to use your rich imagination.

horror movie

 Watch the videos and answer the following questions.

Video 1

 Question

According to the man in the video, how much does the little grey rock cost?

 **Vocabulary** ▼

brink	/briŋk/	*n.*	（……的）边缘
deposit	/di'pɔzit/	*n.*	矿床，矿藏
diplomatic	/ˌdiplə'mætik/	*adj.*	外交的；策略的
indigenous	/in'didʒənəs/	*adj.*	土生土长的
Kansas	/'kænzəs/		美国堪萨斯州
marine	/mə'riːn/	*n.*	海军陆战队士兵
re-locate	/riː 'ləukeit/	*vt.*	搬迁，迁移
savage	/'sævidʒ/	*adj.*	野蛮的，蒙昧的

Questions

What is the man talking about?

What do you know about the company?

Vocabulary ▼

convert	/kən'vəːt/	*vt.*	（使）转变，（使）转化
digital	/'didʒitəl/	*adj.*	数码的
enable	/i'neibl/	*vt.*	使能够
monitor	/'mɔnitə/	*n.*	显示屏

Questions

What technology is used in this film?

How do they use the technology?

Vocabulary ▼

astound	/ə'staund/	*vt.*	使震惊，使大吃一惊
cliff	/klif/	*n.*	悬崖；峭壁
compress	/kəm'pres/	*vt.*	压紧，压缩
enhance	/in'hɑːns/	*vt.*	提高，增加，加强
gorgeous	/'gɔːdʒəs/	*adj.*	非常漂亮的，华美的
mirror	/'mirə/	*vt.*	反映，反射，映照
phenomenal	/fi'nɔmənəl/	*adj.*	非凡的
spectacular	/spek'tækjulə/	*adj.*	壮观的，雄伟的

Ⅲ Work in groups.

Will 3-D movies take the place of traditional movies in the future? Why?
Discuss with your partners, and choose a representative to report to the
whole class.

Nothing in the world is difficult for one who sets his mind to it.

Text

3-D Movies Today

Everybody talks about the 3-D technology, and Hollywood has invested millions of dollars in 3-D cinemas. 3-D movies are well established in cinemas nowadays. In 2009, 3-D movies had a 10-percent market share.

What on earth is 3-D movie? In fact, a 3-D movie is a motion picture that enhances the illusion. Special projection hardware and eyewear are used to provide the illusion of depth when viewing the film. 3-D movies have existed in some form since 1890. Nonetheless, 3-D movies were featured in the 1950s in American cinema, and later experienced a worldwide resurgence in the 1980s and 1990s driven by IMAX high-end theaters and Disney themed venues. 3-D movies became more and more successful throughout 2000-2010. The most successful film of all times is *Avatar* which was filmed in 3-D in December 2009 and January 2010.

3-D movies have made such stir that many families are planning to enjoy the home 3-D movie viewing experience with their children. Is watching a movie in 3-D really that much better?

The answer to this question really depends on you and your family's love for watching movies. If family movie night is something you value, or if you are just really into cool home theater technology, a 3-D TV is a must. Go to your local home theater store and let them give you a demo. You will be impressed. In fact, you may save money on going out to the theater, since everyone will want to wait and see the movie on the 3-D TV at home.

What about young children, will they enjoy watching 3-D movies at home? Even when the movie is great and the glasses are just their size, most very young children just don't keep the glasses on and end up losing interest or watching a fuzzy movie. If your kids are old enough to keep the glasses on their faces, they will be able to enjoy 3-D movies with the rest of the family. Of course, this ability to keep the glasses on depends on the child's age and personality.

But anyway, 3-D has been an important part of movie, and this is just the beginning. In the future, the stirring 4-D movies will make you both astonishing and pleasant.

(376 words)

New Words

astonishing	/ə'stɔniʃiŋ/	*adj.* 惊人的；令人惊讶的
demo	/'deməu/	*n.* 演示；样本唱片
depth	/depθ/	*n.* 深度；深奥
enhance	/in'hɑːns, -hæns/	*vt.* 提高；加强；增加
establish	/i'stæbliʃ/	*vt.* 建立；创办；安置
exist	/ig'zist/	*vi.* 存在；生存；生活；继续存在
existence	/ig'zistəns/	*n.* 存在；生存；生活；存在物
eyewear	/'ai,wɛə/	*n.* 眼镜；眼镜防护；护目镜
feature	/'fiːtʃə/	*n.* 特色，特征　*vt.* 特写；以……为特色
fuzzy	/'fʌzi/	*adj.* 模糊的；失真的；有绒毛的
illusion	/i'ljuːʒən/	*n.* 幻觉，错觉；错误的观念或信仰

kid		n. 儿童　v. 开玩笑
must		n. 必须的条件，不可缺少的东西
nonetheless	/ˌnʌnðə'les/	conj. 尽管如此，但是
personality	/ˌpɜːsə'næləti/	n. 个性；品格；名人
projection	/prəu'dʒekʃən/	n. 投射；规划；突出
resurgence	/ri'sɜːdʒəns/	n. 复活；再现；再起
stir	/stɜː/	n. 搅拌；轰动　vt. 搅拌；激起；惹起
stirring	/'stɜːriŋ/	adj. 激动人心的；活跃的
themed	/θiːmd/	adj. 以……为主题的
venue	/'venjuː/	n. 场地，场馆

Phrases & Expressions

be into...	对……很有兴趣，极喜欢；懂得
depend on	取决于；依赖于
end up	结束；死亡
even when	即使当
motion picture	电影
on earth	究竟

Proper Nouns

Avatar	电影《阿凡达》

Focus on

establish experience enhance feature stir illusion astonishing nonetheless personality depend on end up

Study Independently

You are required to study independently the words and sentences given. Discuss what you have learned and think over the usages in the text.

establish

1. They decided to **establish** a new research center.
2. The police **established** that she was innocent.
3. Our hope is to **establish** mutually beneficial trading relations between us.
4. He **established** himself as a leading surgeon.
5. We should help the child develop self-esteem and **establish** self-confidence.

experience

1. Karl has **experience** in running a school.
2. He **experienced** all kinds of hardships.
3. It was an unforgettable **experience**.
4. All genuine knowledge originates in direct **experience.**
5. Children need to **experience** things for themselves in order to learn from them.

stir

1. She **stirred** her coffee with a plastic spoon.
2. A gentle breeze **stirred** the curtains.
3. He hadn't **stirred** from his chair all morning.
4. Looking at the photographs **stirred** childhood memories of the long hot summers.
5. The incident **stirred** students to protest.
6. Plans for the motorway caused quite a **stir** among locals.

feature

1. An important **feature** of Van Gogh's paintings is their bright colours.
2. Striped tails are a common **feature** of many animals.

3. The magazine makes a **feature** of children's stories.
4. Her mouth is her best **feature**.
5. Wet weather is a **feature** in Scotland.
6. The exhibition **features** paintings by Picasso.
7. The magazine is **featuring** his articles.

Practicing & Developing

Comprehension

(I) Choose the best answer to each of the following questions.

1. Which of the following is true about 3-D movies?
   A. 3-D movies did not exist until 1950s.
   B. 3-D movies become very successful in recent years.
   C. 3-D movies were very popular in the 1970s.
   D. Not many people watch 3-D movies in cinemas.

2. What contributed to the worldwide resurgence of 3-D movies in the 1980s?
   A. 3-D TV.
   B. Special projection hardware.
   C. IMAX high-end theaters.
   D. Home theater technology.

3. If you want to enjoy the home 3-D movies with your family, you need to _____.
   A. buy a 3-D TV   B. inquire the expert
   C. check the website   D. save some money

4. What enables young children to enjoy watching 3-D movies at home?
   A. The glasses are comfortable to wear.
   B. The movies are enjoyable and interesting.
   C. They enjoy watching movies with the family.
   D. They can keep the glasses on their faces.

5. What is the passage mainly about?

A. IMAX high-end theaters.　　B. 3-D home theater.

C. Home theater technology.　　D. Home theater future.

Vocabulary and Structure

II Make the best choice to fill in each blank.

1. We have _____ diplomatic relations with many countries.

A. existed　　B. established　　C. impressed　　D. enhanced

2. Many laws of nature actually _____ in nature though they have not yet been discovered.

A. exist　　B. establish　　C. impress　　D. experience

3. He has 5 years' working _____ in administration.

A. feature　　B. illusion　　C. experience　　D. personality

4. Passing the English examination should _____ your chance of getting the post.

A. experience　　B. establish　　C. impress　　D. enhance

5. The prosperity of society _____ political stability and economic development.

A. ends up　　B. decides on　　C. depends on　　D. substitutes for

6. At dinner we usually begin with soup and _____ with fruit.

A. end up　　B. set out　　C. take on　　D. go over

7. People had bought these houses under the _____ that their value would keep on rising.

A. sense　　B. illusion　　C. feature　　D. imagination

8. The experiment failed. _____, it was worth making.

A. Nevertheless　　B. Moreover　　C. Besides　　D. Therefore

9. His visit to this island country created no small _____ in the diplomatic world.

A. illusion　　B. personality　　C. experience　　D. stir

10. Some people think that environment shape _____.

A. feature　　B. experience　　C. personality　　D. illusion

Ⅲ **Fill in each blank with the right form of the word given in the bracket.**

1. The excellent performance of the freshman gives a good _____ (impress) to the boss.

2. When _____ (view) the photos taken by FMO project, I spotted an FMO and report it at once.

3. He's a man who can be _____ (depend) upon in a crisis.

4. His _____ (stir) speech heated the audience's imagination.

5. If you don't eat less, you'll end up _____ (look) like a whale!

6. I respect him and admire his ability _____ (remain) cool in face of danger.

7. His second novel _____ (establish) his fame as a writer.

8. The packing must be strong enough _____ (withstand) rough handling.

9. We enjoy _____ (see) the glorious beams of the rising sun.

10. The organization was brought into _____ (exist) in 1980.

Ⅳ **Find the items equivalent to those given in Chinese in the table below.**

A. three-dimensional film

B. science fiction film

C. film producer

D. documentary film

E. musical film

F. news film

G. detective film

H. colour film

I. sound film

J. silent film

K. operatic film

L. film script

M. advertising film

N. shoot a film

O. horror film

P. wide-screen film

Q. international film festival

R. action film

S. film studio

T. feature film

U. release a film

V. comic film

Example: (F) 新闻片 (R) 动作片

1. ( ) 科幻片	( ) 纪录片
2. ( ) 侦探片	( ) 恐怖片
3. ( ) 故事片	( ) 喜剧片
4. ( ) 制片人	( ) 制片厂
5. ( ) 拍摄电影	( ) 发行影片

 Choose the best translation.

1. This course will enhance your leadership skills, not only in your current position but throughout your career.

   A. 本课程会提高你的领导技能，无论在目前的职位，还是在整个职业生涯中。

   B. 本课程将提高你的领导能力，不是在目前的职位，而是在整个职业生涯中。

   C. 本课程虽然提高了你目前的领导能力，但它会贯穿你的整个职业生涯。

   D. 本课程会提高你目前的领导技能，这种能力将贯穿你的整个职业生涯。

2. He shows respect for all employees, regardless of gender, race, religion or personality.

   A. 他尊重所有的雇主，不管其性别、种族、宗教信仰或特点如何。

   B. 他尊重所有的雇员，虽然其性别、种族、宗教信仰或性格各异。

   C. 他尊重所有的雇员，不管其性别、种族、宗教信仰或个性如何。

   D. 他尊重所有的雇主，不在意其性别、种族、宗教信仰或特点如何。

3. Impressed by the courage and good fellowship of his shipmates, he takes up a life of adventure.

   A. 在水手们的勇气和良好的伙伴关系的感召下，他开始了他的冒险生涯。

   B. 水手们勇敢和良好的伙伴使他有勇气开始他的冒险生涯。

   C. 水手们的勇气和良好的伙伴关系鼓舞了他，他开始了他的冒险生涯。

   D. 水手们的勇气和良好的伙伴关系给他留下深刻印象，他便开始了他的冒险生涯。

4. The progress and development of a society depends on how well human dignity is maintained and how much human value is realized.

   A. 一切社会的发展和进步，取决于人的尊严的维护和价值的实现。

   B. 一切社会的发展和进步，决定了人的尊严的维护和价值的发挥。

C . 社会的发展和进步是以人的尊严的维护和价值的发挥为基础的。

D . 一个社会的发展和进步离不开人的尊严的维护和价值的实现。

5. If you keep contact with the school even when they have refused you financial aid, you may get it later because of the unexpected money.

A. 即使学校已经拒绝了你的经济资助申请，如果你和学校保持联系，你或许会因为一些意外资金而最终得到资助。

B. 如果学校已经拒绝了你的经济资助申请，即使和学校保持联系，你也不会因为一些意外资金而最终得到资助。

C. 如果学校已经拒绝了你的经济资助申请，你要和学校保持联系，你或许会得到意想不到的资助。

D. 如果你和学校保持联系，虽然学校已经拒绝了你的经济资助申请，你或许会得到意想不到的资助。

Reading

The Best and Worst 3-D Movies of All Time

Find a list of the best and worst 3-D movies of all time! The best 3-D movies add depth and texture to stories that are already good, yet somehow, the worst 3-D movies just remind the viewer more forcefully how awful they are. But anyway the viewer has a heightened experience. Enjoy this list of the best and worst 3-D movies on your new 3-D TV.

The Worst 3-D Movies

Unless you're a girl aged 11 to 13, or younger, you'll agree that *Jonas Brothers: The 3-D Concert Experience* ranks among the worst, although the movie shows complicated 3-D effects.

A lot of the 3-D effects were made to look as if they were coming right off the screen into the audience. It's maybe not the worst movie out there, *but definitely a contender for the worst 3-D movie.*

Even though there were plenty of people who considered *The Adventures of Sharkboy and Lava Girl 3-D* the worst 3-D movie ever, there were a handful that had zeal in their love for it.

The Best 3-D Movies

Polar Express 3-D is dark, dreamy, and full of innocent wonder. Some haters criticized the addition of several characters not in the book, but since the book was only about 30 pages long, it required some expansion to get it to movie length. You could almost watch it with no sound and get a wonderful experience because the artwork is so beautiful. It's a 3-D dreamscape that anyone from age 3 to 100 will love.

You know how smug it feels to tell someone, "Be careful what you wish for!" Well, that's the underlying premise of *Coraline*, a 2009 movie that didn't get nearly the attention it deserved. This movie has that enchanting-but-slightly-frightening feel of other great movies like *The Nightmare Before Christmas*.

Alfred Hitchcock's *Dial M for Murder* stars Grace Kelly as the Hitchcock Blonde, and it is impossible to do justice to the plot in just a few words. Whether you can see it in 3-D or not, this is one of the all-time great 3-D movies, and if you haven't seen it, you're really missing out.

And of course, no discussion of 3-D movies is complete without mention of *AVATAR*. Based on ticket sales alone, it is a contender for not just one of the best 3-D movies, but the best all-around movie of many years.

(409 words)

New Words

awful	/'ɔːful/	*adj.* 可怕的，庄严的
contender	/kən'tendə/	*n.* 竞争者；争夺者
definitely	/'definitli/	*adv.* 清楚地，当然；明确地，肯定地
depth	/depθ/	*n.* 深度；深奥
dreamscape	/'driːmskeip/	*n.* 梦幻景象，幻景
enchanting	/in'tʃɑːntiŋ, en-/	*adj.* 迷人的；妩媚的
expansion	/ik'spænʃən/	*n.* 膨胀；阐述；扩张物
handful	/'hændful/	*n.* 少数；一把；棘手事
hater	/'heitə/	*n.* 怀恨者
heighten	/'haitən/	*v.* 提高，升高
innocent	/'inəsənt/	*n.* 天真的人；笨蛋
premise	/'premis/	*n.* 前提；上述各项
smug	/smʌg/	*n.* 书呆子；自命不凡的家伙
star	/stɑː/	*n.* 星，明星　*vt.* 由……主演　*vi.* 担任主角
texture	/'tekstʃə/	*n.* 质地；纹理；结构；本质，实质
underlying	/ˌʌndə'laiiŋ/	*adj.* 潜在的；根本的；在下面的；优先的
zeal	/ziːl/	*n.* 热情；热心；热诚

Phrases & Expressions

miss out	错过；遗漏；省略
pick up	捡起；获得；收拾
rank among	跻身于；属于之列

 **Exercises**

Reading Comprehension

Choose the best answer to each of the following questions or complete the statements.

1. Which of the following is considered the worst 3-D movie?
   A. *Dial M for Murder*.
   B. *Polar Express 3-D*.
   C. *The Nightmare Before Christmas*.
   D. *Jonas Brothers: The 3-D Concert Experience*.

2. People have different reactions to _____.
   A. *Dial M for Murder*
   B. *The Nightmare Before Christmas*
   C. *The Adventrures of Sharkboy and Lava Girl*
   D. *Jonas Brothers: The 3-D Concert Experience*

3. The sentence "...but definitely a contender for the worst 3-D movie" in Paragraph 3 suggests that _____.
   A. it is the best 3-D movie
   B. it is the worst 3-D movie
   C. it is better than the worst 3-D movies
   D. it is by no means the worst 3-D movie

4. Which of the following is NOT true according to the passage?
   A. Both the best and worst 3-D movies give the viewers a heightened experience.
   B. A lot of 3-D effects were used in *Jonas Brothers: The 3-D Concert Experience*.
   C. *Coraline* gives us the same feeling as *The Nightmare Before Christmas*.
   D. Many people enjoy watching *The Adventrures of Sharkboy and Lava Girl*.

5. What is the author's attitude towards *AVATAR*?
   A. Critical.
   B. Positive.
   C. Negative.
   D. Disappointed.

Grammar

动名词 *(the Gerund)*

Pretest

Choose the best answer to each of the following questions.

1. She never dreams of _____ for her to be sent abroad.
   A. there to be   B. there being a chance
   C. there be a chance   D. being a chance

2. I can't help _____ about the school years when we stayed together.
   A. to think   B. thinking   C. and think   D. being thought

3. We are looking forward to _____ the film _____ next week.
   A. seeing; shown   B. see; shown
   C. seeing; to show   D. see; to show

4. John was annoyed. He couldn't bear _____ like that before the whole class.
   A. making fun of   B. being laughed at
   C. made fun of   D. being made fun

5. _____ computer games cost the boy a lot of time.
   A. To have played   B. Playing   C. Played   D. Having played

6. I stopped _____ things in his shop after I found the goods of bad quality.
   A. buying   B. buy   C. to buy   D. bought

7. _____ to sunlight for a long time will do harm to our skin.
   A. Exposed   B. Having exposed
   C. After being exposed   D. Being exposed

动名词兼有动词和名词的特征，有时态和语态的变化。

一、动名词的作用

动名词在句中可以做主语、表语、宾语、定语等。

1. 做主语

Seeing is believing. 眼见为实。

当动名词做主语时，我们常用先行词 it 做形式主语，尤其在下列结构中：

It is useless (no use, no good, no harm, fun) doing... 做……没有用处（没有好处，没有坏处，有趣）

It is a waste of time doing... 做……浪费时间

It is worthwhile doing... 做……是值得的

此时，要把真正的主语动名词放到句尾。例如：

It is no use persuading him to join us. 劝他加入我们是没有用的。

在 **There + be + no + V-ing** 句型中，动词要用 ing 形式。如：

There is no joking about such serious matters. 对这种严肃的事情开不得玩笑。

2. 做宾语

（1）做动词 / 动词短语的宾语

● 某些动词后只能用动名词做宾语，不能用不定式。常见的此类动词有：advise, allow, permit, avoid, consider, enjoy, finish, imagine, include, keep, mind, miss, delay, practice, resist, suggest 等。如：

You should practice speaking English every day. 你应该每天都练习说英语。

● 有些动词短语后面也要求跟动名词做宾语。这样的短语动词常见的有：feel like，give up，go on，object/objection to，put off，keep on，insist on，leave off，look forward to，think of，can't help，be/get used to，spend...in，have difficulty in, have trouble/a hard time in, confess to 等。如：

I look forward to seeing my friend soon. 我盼望很快见到我的朋友。

● 有些动词既可带动名词也可带不定式做宾语，但表达的意思不同：

forget/remember doing sth. 忘记 / 记得做过……
forget/remember to do sth. 忘记 / 记得做……

try doing sth. 尝试做……
try to do sth. 努力、设法做……

{ mean doing sth. 意味着……
{ mean to do sth. 打算做……

{ stop doing sth. 停止做……
{ stop to do sth. 停下来去做……

如：

Do you mean to tell me you didn't post it? 你打算告诉我你没有寄出吗？

If you haven't done that, it'll mean waiting and waiting again. 如果你还没有做那件事，就意味着要一等再等。

He tried to write better. 他尽量写得好些。

He tried writing with a brush. 他尝试着用毛笔写字。

（2）做介词的宾语

We are thinking of making a plan to solve the problem. 我们正想着制订一个计划来解决这个问题。

（3）做形容词的宾语

The music is worth listening to. 这种音乐值得听。

3. 做表语

动名词做表语时句子主语常是表示无生命的事物的名词或 what 引导的名词性从句。表语动名词与主语通常是对等的关系，表示主语的内容时，主语、表语可互换位置。如：

His hobby is listening to music. 他的爱好是听音乐。

(Listening to music is his hobby.)

动名词和不定式都可做表语，动名词表示一般行为，不定式表示具体的某次动作，特别是将来的动作，如：

Her job is taking care of the children. 她的工作是照顾孩子们。

The job we should do this afternoon is to clean the house. 我们今天下午要做的工作是清扫房子。

4. 做定语

动名词做定语往往表示被修饰词的某种用途。如：

washing machine = a machine used for washing

building materials = materials used for building

二、动名词的时态和语态（以动词 do 为例）

时态＼语态	主动语态	被动语态
一般式	doing	being done
完成式	having done	having been done

1. 动名词一般式：**doing**

　　表示的通常是一般性动作，即不是明确地发生在过去、现在或将来的动作，或是与谓语动词所表示的动作同时发生的动作。如：

　　Being careless brings her a lot of trouble. 粗心给她带来了很多麻烦。

2. 动名词的完成式：**having done**

　　表示的动作发生在谓语动词动作之前。如：

　　I don't remember having seen him before. 我不记得以前见过他。

3. 动名词的被动语态：**being done/ having been done**

　　当逻辑主语同时也是动名词动作的承受者时，动名词用被动语态。

　　（1）一般式表示的动作与谓语动词动作同时发生，或在其前发生。如：

　　I don't like being treated that way in public. 在公共场合下，我不喜欢受到那种方式的对待。

　　（2）它的完成式表示的动作发生在谓语动词之前。如：

　　We are all very pleased at your having been accepted as a member of the club. 你被接收为这个俱乐部的会员，我们都很高兴。

Practice

　　Identify *the gerund* in the text. (The reference key can be found in this unit.)

Practical Writing and Reading

Letter of Recommendation

无论是求学还是求职，推荐信都起着至关重要的作用。推荐信要写得全面、详细、实事求是，以达到推荐的目的和要求。开头要写清楚推荐人和申请人之间的关系以及推荐信的意图。中间展开介绍申请人的一些情况，如学习能力、成绩、论文、排名，或者学历学位、专业特长、沟通能力、领导能力、团队合作能力等。中间这部分目的是使对方了解申请人，对申请人产生好感，从而达到推荐的目的。结尾总结说明申请人值得被推荐，希望对方能考虑接收或录用申请人。

写推荐信要注意实事求是，尽量避免对任何人都适用的套语，要力求反映申请人的特点。介绍申请人情况应详细具体，不要泛泛而谈。

推荐信的格式同样包括：信头 heading，信内地址 inside address，称呼语 salutation，正文 body of the letter，结尾谦词 complimentary close，签名 Signature，附件 Enclosure (Enc.)

常见开头句子：

(1) I have the honor to introduce to you my best friend Dr. Kong Wen.

(2) It gives me much pleasure to introduce Mr. Black.

(3) I am pleased to write this letter of recommendation for Helen Clark, one of my favorite students and who is currently teaching in for admission to your esteemed university.

(4) It is my pleasure to recommend to you my colleague, Mr. ...

(5) I am glad to recommend Mr. Wang, one of my colleagues to you.

常见正文句子：

(1) He is competent and reliable, and we can thoroughly recommend him.

(2) He is intelligent, honest, and hard-working.

(3) We have found him a most capable and responsible worker and our relations with him have been entirely cordial.

(4) She has special interest in the study of languages and is also most interested in the means of communication.

(5) He has consistently ranked high in his class.

常见结尾句子：

(1) Please accept my letter of recommendation.

(2) I recommend him highly for your consideration.

(3) In closing, based on my experience working with her, I can unreservedly recommend her to you.

Sample:

June 18, 2010

Thomas Clark

Dean of Software Engineering

School of Computer

5544 Casino Way

El Cajon, CA

Dear Mr. Clark,

I am writing you this letter of recommendation in support of Mr. John Lee. It is his desire to attend the School of Computer and advance his knowledge within your Software Engineering program. John has a proven track record with his grades as well as his attendance. As a professor here at Information Engineering School, I am impressed by only a few outstanding students each year, and John is one of those students who stand above the rest. I am proud to recommend him for your program.

John is one of my top students, with grades that place him within the top two percent. John excels on all courses as well as projects. His last project describing a secure Internet using relay nodes to server attacks is a great example of his unique thinking. When we first met six years ago, I knew that John was a unique student, with great aptitude, ability and potential.

John's academic records certainly qualify him for your program, and his thesis work will provide a unique perspective to your organization. Please accept my letter of recommendation, and if you have any question, please feel free to contact me.

Sincerely yours,

Manuel Cirenia

 *Practice*

Task 1

根据下面题目要求，写一封自荐信。

你是北京联合大学一名学生王楠，现在向 Black 教授写一封信推荐你自己。

内容包括：

（1）你申请计算机科学硕士学位。

（2）你在校期间成绩优异，英语突出，聪明、勤奋、为人诚实。

（3）若对方需要更多信息，请直接联系你。

Task 2

Directions: The following is a *recommendation letter*. After reading it, you are required to complete the outline below it (No. 1 through No. 5). You should write your answer briefly (in no more than 3 words).

Sept. 7, 2010

Dear Mrs. Villas,

It gives me much pleasure to recommend Joan Austin to you. She has been teaching English at our university for nearly two years. During these two years, she did a credible job giving classes in Spoken English, English Listening and Intensive English. In total, she taught these subjects to four different classes. She showed a good grasp of the materials and was able to develop an excellent rapport with her students. She was one of the most popular teachers at our university.

Unfortunately, her family will move to your city, and Joan has to resign from her present teaching job. We will truly miss her.

Joan is a high energy self-starter who quickly assumes responsibility and is not afraid to face new challenges and situations. She is also very personable. Not only did she get along well with her students, she was also popular with the faculty.

As vice-principal, I would definitely rehire Joan given the opportunity. I recommend her highly for your consideration.

Sincerely,

Crismon Green

Vice-principal

Relationship between the writer and Joan: _____1_____

Joan's past job: _____2_____

Reason for Joan's resignation: _____3_____ will move to another city.

Reasons for recommendation:

 a. She was one of the most popular teachers.

 b. She is a _____4_____ self-starter.

 c. She dares to face new _____5_____.

 d. She is also very personable.

Task 3

Directions: The following is a *recommendation letter*. After reading it, you should give brief answers to the 5 questions (No. 1 through No. 5). The answers (in no more than 3 words) should be written after the corresponding numbers.

March 12, 2010

Mr. Robert Phillips

Manager, Marketing Division

Allied Technologies

110 Friars Road

Stamford, CA 06907

Dear Mr. Phillips,

This is in response to your recent request for a letter of recommendation for Linda Vista who worked for me up until one year ago.

Linda worked under my direct supervision at Michael Telecom for a period of five years ending in January 2009. During that period, I had the great pleasure of seeing her blossom from a junior marketing trainee at the beginning into a fully functioning Marketing Program Coordinator in her final two years with the company.

Linda is a hard-working self-starter who invariably understands exactly what a project is all about from the outset, and how to get it done quickly and effectively. During her two years in the marketing coordinator position, I cannot remember an instance in which she missed a major deadline. Linda is also a resourceful, creative, and solution-oriented person who was frequently able to come up with new and innovative approaches to her assigned projects. On the interpersonal side, Linda has superior written and verbal communication skills. She gets along extremely well with staff under her supervision, as well as colleagues at her own level. She is highly respected, as both a person and a professional, by colleagues, employees, suppliers, and customers alike.

In closing, as detailed above, based on my experience working with her, I can unreservedly recommend Linda to you for any intermediate or senior marketing position. If you would like further elaboration, feel free to call me at 611-559-559.

Sincerely,

Shaun Katzman

Director, Marketing and Sales

1. Who requested for the letter of recommendation?
   _____.

2. What is the relationship between the writer and Linda?
   _____ worked for _____ for five years.

3. What kind of person is Linda ?
   Linda is a _____ self-starter, a resourceful, creative, and _____ person.

4. Does Linda get along well with her colleagues?
   _____.

5. What position is Linda recommended for?
   The writer recommends Linda for any _____ marketing position.

Task 4

Translate the following passage.

Find a list of the best and worst 3-D movies of all time! The best 3-D movies add depth and texture to stories that are already good, yet somehow, the worst 3-D movies just remind the viewer more forcefully how awful they are.

_____

_____

_____

Key to the grammar practice:

1. Is *watching* a movie in 3-D really that much better?

2. The answer to this question really depends on you and your family's love for *watching* movies.

3. In fact, you may save money on *going* out to the theater, since everyone will want to wait and see the movie on the 3-D TV at home.

4. What about young children, will they enjoy *watching* 3-D movies at home?

5. Even when the movie is great and the glasses are just their size, most very young children just don't keep the glasses on and end up *losing* interest or *watching* a fuzzy movie.

Music

Listening

Dialogue One   Attending A Concert

Words and Expressions (Ⅰ)

appeal	/ə'pi:l/	*v.*	对……有吸引力
attend a concert			听音乐会
classical music			古典乐
folk song			民歌
melodious	/mə'ləudiːəs/	*adj.*	悦耳的，旋律优美的
National Center for the Performing Arts			国家大剧院
orchestral	/ɔ:'kestrəl/	*adj.*	管弦乐队（演奏）的
quartet	/kwɔ:'tet/	*n.*	四重奏；四重唱
tenor solo			男高音独唱

Patterns (Ⅰ)

Learn the following sentence patterns to practice listening and speaking.

1. —**How** did **you like** Miss William's singing?

   —She sang very well, I thought.

2. —**What type of music do you like the best?**

   —**I like** classical music **best**.

or —**I have a special liking for** classical music.

3. —How did you like the rest of the concert?

   —**I like** the tenor solo **fairly well**.

4. —**What do you say to that?**

   —American pop music doesn't **appeal to** me.

 Exercise (I)

This section is to test your ability to understand Dialogue One. There are five questions for Dialogue One. After the dialogue, you should decide on the correct answer from the four choices marked A, B, C and D given below.

1. Which person did not attend the concert last night?

   A. Li Hua.   B. Laura.

   C. Jack.   D. George.

2. What did Miss William sing at the concert?

   A. A pop song.   B. A folk song.

   C. A classical song.   D. Both A and B.

3. What type of music does Laura like best?

   A. Pop music.   B. Classical music.

   C. Orchestral music.   D. Rock and Roll.

4. Which expression is NOT true about American pop music?

   A. Laura does not like American pop music.

   B. American pop music is played all over the world.

   C. It is enjoyed by people of all ages in many countries.

   D. It is popular because of its slow pace.

5. How many programs were there in the concert according to Dialogue One?

   A. Four.   B. Five.   C. Six.   D. Seven.

Dialogue Two   A Devoted Fan

Words and Expressions (Ⅱ)

after all	毕竟
as well	也
be described as	被描述成
one's favorite	某人的最爱
pop music	流行音乐
remind sb. of	使某人想起……
sing along with	跟着……一起唱
translate...into	把……翻译成……

Patterns (Ⅱ)

Learn the following sentence patterns to practice listening and speaking.

1. —**What kind of music** do you usually listen to?

   —Well, a wide range of music, but Jay Chou's songs **are my favorite**.

2. It is special because its lyrics are like traditional Chinese poems and it **reminds you of** ancient Chinese life.

3. —Have you heard of TVXQ, the Korean singing group?

   —Well, they work hard and they are very modest.

4. How do you enjoy their songs?

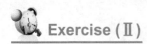

Exercise (Ⅱ)

Listen to Dialogue Two and complete it with what you hear.

Nana: Hi, Lee, any plan for the weekend?

Lee: Just staying at home and listening to music.

Nana: What kind of music do you usually listen to?

Lee: Well, a wide range of music, but Jay Chou's songs are my favorite, especially his ____1____ songs.

Nana: How can ____2____ be described as traditional?

Lee: Well, in each of Jay Chou's albums he will include a special song. It is special because its lyrics are like traditional Chinese poems and it reminds you of ancient Chinese life. That's why the songs are considered to be traditional Chinese style.

Nana: Wow, you certainly know a lot about Jay Chou.

Lee: Sure! What kind of music do you like?

Nana: Me? I like pop music as well. But I like Korean singers. Have you heard of TVXQ, the Korean singing group?

Lee: I have heard of them, but not ____3____.

Nana: Well, they work hard and they are very modest. They even said that they had not ____4____ when they won the title of "The best singer group in Asia".

Lee: Wow, that's impressive. How do you enjoy their songs?

Nana: Their fans have translated their lyrics into Chinese. Besides, I'm learning Korean so that one day I can sing ____5____ their songs.

Lee: You are surely a devoted fan.

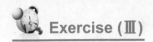

Exercise (Ⅲ)

Creative Thinking

Enjoy a part of the film *Barbie: The Diamond Castle* and discuss what you just watched. You are required to act it out.

Speaking

Ⅰ Work in pairs: Make a dialogue.

Please choose one of the following pictures, and then according to the sentence patterns you have just learnt, make up a dialogue with your partner. You are encouraged to use your rich imagination.

Ⅱ Watch the videos and answer the following questions.

🔍 **Vocabulary** ▼

crown	/kraun/	*vt.*	为……加冕
explode	/iks'pləud/	*v.*	激增，迅速扩大
fad	/fæd/	*n.*	一时的流行
Mississippi	/ˌmisi'sipi/		美国密西西比州
slip	/slip/	*v.*	滑，溜，滑倒
tune	/tjuːn/	*n.*	曲调，曲子
witness	/'witnis/	*vt.*	亲眼看见，目击

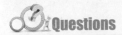**Questions**

Who is the video about?

What happened in 1956 according to the video?

fairytale	/ˈfɛəriteil/	*adj.*	童话式的
identify	/aiˈdentifai/	*v.*	等同于
inspire	/inˈspaiə/	*vt.*	赋予某人灵感; 启迪
make-believe	/ˈmeikbiˈliːv/	*adj.*	虚构的；虚幻的
ranch	/rɑːntʃ/	*n.*	牧场，大农场
slice	/slais/	*n.*	部分；份

Questions

Where is Michael Jackson's home "Neverland" located?

Where does the name "Neverland" come from?

Vocabulary

album	/'ælbəm/	*n.*	音乐专辑，歌曲专辑
debut	/'deibuː/	*n.*	（演员、运动员）首次亮相
eardrum	/'iəˌdrʌm/	*n.*	鼓膜，耳膜
scream	/skriːm/	*v.*	尖叫

Questions

Who is the first artist in video history to have four No.1 hits in her debut album?

What does she listen to according to her answer in the interview?

III Learn an English song.

Are you a music-lover? Who is your favorite singer?

The following song is an American country song.

El Condor Pasa

I'd rather be a sparrow than a snail.
Yes I would.
If I could,
I surely would.

I'd rather be a hammer than a nail.
Yes I would.
If I only could,
I surely would.

Away, I'd rather sail away
Like a swan that's here and gone.
A man gets tied to the ground,
He gives the world its saddest sound,
Its saddest sound.

I'd rather be a forest than a street.
Yes I would.
If I could,
I surely would.

I'd rather feel the earth beneath my feet.
Yes I would.
If I only could,
I surely would.

Away, I'd rather sail away
Like a swan that's here and gone.
A man gets tied to the ground,
He gives the world its saddest sound,
Its saddest sound.

When in Rome, do as the Romans do.

Text

Americans' Taste in Music

James Fenimore Cooper, an early American writer, once said, "Americans are almost ignorant of the art of music." If that was once true, you would never know it today. Most Americans—even those without a musical bone in their bodies—have a favorite style of music. Many people enjoy classical and folk music from around the world, but other popular music styles were "made in the U.S. A.".

Country and western music lies close to the heart of many Americans. This style originated among country folks in the southern and western United States. Country music tells *down-to-earth* stories about love and life's hardships. Guitars, banjos and violins give country music its characteristic sound. The home of country music is Nashville, Tennessee—Music City U.S.A. Country music even has its own theme park called "Opryland" where you can enjoy music shows and fun rides.

Jazz music, developed by African-Americans in the late 1800s, allows performers to freely express their emotions and musical skills. Instead of just playing the melody, jazz musicians improvise different tunes using the same chords.

The 1950s saw the development of an explosive new music style: rock 'n' roll. Performers like Elvis Presley and songs like Bill Haley's "Rock Around the Clock" made rock music widely popular. This powerful music style addresses issues like love, sex, drugs, politics and death. Often it rebels against the accepted values of society. Rock concerts, featuring loud music and sometimes weird stage acts, have become a major part of the American youth culture. Music videos on television have spread the message of rock to the far corners of the globe.

And the beat goes on. Pop music represents popular styles. "Golden oldies" from the past bring back pleasant memories for many. Rap music, which burst onto the music scene in the 1970s, is actually more like a rhyming chant. Rappers give a strong—sometimes vulgar—message about life on the streets.

In America, music is a shared experience. People grow up with piano lessons, chorus classes and marching band practices. They can talk about their tastes in music.

(355 words)

New Words

address	/ə'dres/	n. 地址；演讲　vt. 演说；从事
banjo	/'bændʒəu/	n. 班卓琴
chant	/tʃɑːnt, tʃænt/	n. 圣歌；赞美诗
characteristic	/ˌkærəktə'ristik/	n. 特征；特性；特色
chord	/kɔːd/	n. 弦；和弦
chorus	/'kɔːrəs/	n. 合唱队；齐声　vt. 合唱
classical	/'klæsikəl/	n. 古典音乐　adj. 古典的；经典的
down-to-earth	/'dauntə'əːθ/	adj. 实际的；现实的
explosive	/ik'spləusiv/	n. 炸药；爆炸物　adj. 爆炸的；爆炸性的
favorite	/'feivərit/	adj. 最喜爱的；中意的；宠爱的
folk	/fəuk/	n. 民族；亲属（复数）　adj. 民间的
hardship	/'hɑːdʃip/	n. 困苦；苦难；艰难险阻
ignorant	/'ignərənt/	adj. 无知的；愚昧的
ignore	/ig'nɔː/	vt. 驳回诉讼；忽视；不理睬
improvise	/'imprəvaiz/	vt. 即兴创作；即兴表演
melody	/'melədi/	n. 旋律；歌曲；美妙的音乐
origin	/'ɔridʒin, 'ɔː-/	n. 起源；原点；出身；开端
originate	/ə'ridʒəneit/	vt. 引起；创作　vi. 发源；发生；起航
performer	/pə'fɔːmə/	n. 执行者；演奏者
popular	/'pɔpjulə/	adj. 流行的，通俗的；受欢迎的

rap	/ræp/	*vt.* 抢走；轻敲 *vi.* 敲击；交谈 *n.* 说唱乐
rapper	/'ræpə/	*n.* 说唱歌手
rebel	/'rebəl, ri'bel/	*n.* 反叛者；叛徒 *vi.* 反叛；反抗
represent	/,repri'zent/	*vt.* 代表；表现；描绘 *vi.* 代表；提出异议
rhyming	/'raimiŋ/	*n.* 押韵 *adj.* 押韵的
ride	/raid/	*vt.* 骑；乘；控制
theme	/θi:m/	*n.* 主题；主旋律；题目
weird	/wiəd/	*adj.* 怪异的；不可思议的；超自然的
vulgar	/'vʌlgə/	*adj.* 粗俗的；通俗的；本土的

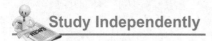

Phrases & Expressions

bring back	拿回来；使……恢复；使……回忆起来
go on	继续；过去；继续下去；发生
grow up	成长，逐渐形成

Focus on

ignorant   originate   address   rebel   popular   favorite   represent
grow up   go on   bring back

 ## Study Independently

You are required to study independently the words and sentences given. Discuss what you have learned and think over the usages in the text.

ignorant

1. She was **ignorant** of this event.

2. I was quite **ignorant** when the earthquake happened.

3. I am **ignorant** in classical music.

4. He is an **ignorant** and uneducated man.

address

1. My email **address** is on my business card.

2. The mayor gave a television **address** yesterday evening.

3. Now, let us invite Ms Jeanne to **address** us.

4. You can **address** me as Doctor.

originate

1. The film **originated** from a novel.

2. Many Christmas traditions **originated** in Germany.

3. Fireworks are said to have **originated** by the Chinese people.

4. The technique was **originated** by an Italian artist.

5. The use of the computer has **originated** many other reforms.

rebel

1. Two of the **rebel** leaders were strung up as a warning to the others.

2. She became a **rebel** when her father was put in prison.

3. We do not want you to **rebel** against your parents.

4. He excited the people to **rebel** against their rulers.

5. The **rebel** army is attempting to subvert the government.

represent

1. Mr. Kobayashi was chosen to **represent** the company at the conference.

2. She decided to **represent** herself (=speak for herself without a lawyer) during the trial.

3. Her greatest ambition was to **represent** her country at the Olympics.

4. Brown areas **represent** deserts on the map.

5. The article **represents** the millionaire as a simple family man.

 Practicing & Developing

𝒞omprehension

 Choose the best answer to each of the following questions.

1. What did James Fenimore Cooper say about the Americans?
   A. They have no taste in music.

B. They have a gift for music.

C. They have their favorite music.

D. They know nothing but American music.

2. Which of the following is NOT mentioned in the passage?

A. Rock music.　　B. Jazz music.　　C. Rap music.　　D. The blues.

3. What does the word "down-to-earth" (Para. 2, Line 3) mean?

A. Practical.　　B. Imaginary.　　C. Idealistic.　　D. Amazing.

4. Which of the following statements is true according to the passage?

A. Both country music and jazz music were developed by African-Americans.

B. The song "Rock Around the Clock" made Elvis Presley widely popular in the US.

C. Rap music is the oldest form of American music developed in the 1800s.

D. Modern inventions have made rock music widely popular around the world.

5. What is the passage mainly about?

A. Different forms of American music.

B. The history of American music.

C. The development of rock and roll.

D. American youth culture.

Vocabulary and Structure

II Make the best choice to fill in each blank.

1. They appear to be _____ of what is going on here.

A. popular　　　B. ignorant　　　C. favorite　　　D. innocent

2. All theories _____ from practice and in turn serve practice.

A. originate　　B. express　　　C. ignore　　　D. represent

3. Please _____ the complaints to the manager, not to me.

A. judge　　　B. address　　　C. benefit　　　D. spread

4. The colonists took up weapons to _____ against the British ruler.

A. develop　　B. express　　　C. rebel　　　D. represent

5. The new type engines _____ high speed, small size and low costs.

A. spread　　　B. develop　　　C. perform　　　D. feature

6. Baseball is very _____ among Americans.

    A. popular   B. favorite   C. pleasant   D. attractive

7. Listening to music is my _____ pastime.

    A. popular   B. favorite   C. likely   D. ignorant

8. Let's discuss the matter out _____ quarreling.

    A. as well as   B. along with   C. in addition to   D. instead of

9. The pictures will instantly _____ happy memories of fun and relaxing times.

    A. come back   B. bring back   C. take up   D. grow up

10. As time _____, many changes took place in our village.

    A. went on   B. brought up   C. worked on   D. turned out

III Fill in each blank with the right form of the word given in the bracket.

1. We are still woefully _____ (ignore) of the causes of this disease.

2. How did the tradition of eating roast turkey on Thanksgiving Day _____ (origin)?

3. He has been playing all afternoon instead of _____ (complete) his work.

4. _____ (feature) small cafes and art shops, the town has regular craft fairs and cultural events.

5. Being one of the six _____ (accept) languages in the UN, English plays a very important role in international affairs.

6. The Internet allows users all over the world _____ (exchange) electronic mail.

7. Sidney Poitier is the first black _____ (perform) in a leading role to winning an Oscar for his role in *Lilies of the Field*.

8. Most of the less developed areas are rich in resources, having great potential for _____ (develop).

9. This easy-to-read guide _____ (address) mainly to those who wish to study abroad.

10. When _____ (complete), the science museum will open to the public next year.

IV Find the items equivalent to those given in Chinese in the table below.

A. feature article   B. feature film

C. popular culture   D. classical music

E. country house   F. popular election

G. theme park   H. folk music

I. classical architecture   J. feature coding

K. theme music   L. popular literature

M. popular science   N. classical literature

O. musical instrument   P. folk custom

Q. music video   R. country music

S. folk culture   T. folk dance

Example: (I)古典建筑 (J) 特征编码

1. ( ) 故事片	( ) 通俗文学
2. ( ) 民间习俗	( ) 主题音乐
3. ( ) 古典文学	( ) 音乐视频
4. ( ) 专题文章	( ) 民间舞蹈
5. ( ) 乐器	( ) 乡间别墅

V Choose the best translation.

1. Even your alarm clock or kitchen coffee machine may have a feature that displays emails that arrived overnight.

   A. 甚至你家的闹钟或厨房的煮咖啡机也可能显示夜间到达的电子邮件。

   B. 甚至你家的闹钟或厨房的煮咖啡机也可能显示收到的电子邮件。

   C. 你家的闹钟或厨房的煮咖啡机的特点是能显示夜间到达的电子邮件。

   D. 你甚至能在闹钟和厨房的煮咖啡机上看到夜里收到的电子邮件。

2. A music student needs as long and as arduous a training to become a performer as a medical student needs to become a doctor.

   A. 一个学习音乐的人要经过长期艰苦的努力成为一名演奏家，一个学医人的要努力成为一名医生。

   B. 一个学习音乐的人经过长期艰苦的努力最终会成为音乐家，一个学医的人最终会成为医生。

   C. 学习音乐的人经过一个漫长而艰苦的过程会成为一名演奏家。同样，学医的人会成为一名医生。

   D. 如同学医的人要成为一名医生一样，学习音乐的人需要长期艰苦的训练才能成为一名演奏家。

3. Not surprisingly, visiting grand houses at a historical point of interest is more popular with adults than with children.

   A. 毫不奇怪，无论成年人还是孩子们都喜欢到历史景点参观豪宅。

   B. 孩子们比成年人更喜欢到历史景点参观豪宅，这一点并不令人奇怪。

   C. 比起孩子们来，到历史景点参观豪宅更受成年人的欢迎，这一点并不令人惊讶。

   D. 一点也不令人惊讶的是，到历史景点参观豪宅的成年人要比孩子们多得多。

4. Intelish is a new artificial language aimed at being the international common language instead of Esperanto.

   A. 国际语是一种以替代世界语作为国际通用语为目标的新的人造语言。

   B. 国际语是一种新的人造语言，它替代了作为国际通用语言的世界语。

   C. 与作为国际通用的世界语一样，国际语是一种新的人造语言。

   D. 国际语是一种新的人造语言，它与世界语一道成为了国际通用语言。

5. He set out to question how life had developed on the earth.

   A. 他试图对地球上的生命是如何产生的那些观点提出质疑。

   B. 他开始对地球上的生命是如何产生的问题提出看法。

   C. 他提出了一个有关地球上生命的发展进化问题。

   D. 他开始思考生命是如何在地球上发展这个问题。

Reading

Pop Music History

In the history of music, the term "pop music" was first used in 1926. It was used to describe "a piece of music having popular appeal". Commercially recorded music, consisting of relatively short and simple songs, is known as "pop music". It is associated with the "rock and roll" style, often tailored for the youth market, *which* utilizes technological innovations to produce new variations on existing themes. Pop music originated in Britain in the mid-1950s, and include such artists as the Beatles, the Rolling Stones, Abba, among others.

If you go through pop music's history, you will notice that pop music has been influenced by other genres of music. Pop music picked up instrumentation from jazz and rock music, vocal harmonies from gospel and soul music, formed from the sentimental ballads, tempo from dance music, support from electronic music and spoken words from rap music. In the 1950s television was introduced and the visual presence of pop stars helped it to gain more popularity. In the 1960s, cheap portable radios were introduced, which allowed teenagers to listen to music outside of the home. By the 1980s MTV favored artists such as Michael Jackson, Prince and Madonna who all had a strong visual appeal. Widespread use of the microphone, multi-track recording, and digital sampling were other technological innovations responsible for the increasing popularity of pop music.

Though pop music had been dominated by the American music industry, other countries have their own form of pop music. In the 1980s video technique was introduced and pop albums became even more popular. The American pop music history has taught us important changes that occurred in the 1960s and 1970s, such as the development of a number of new styles, including heavy metal, soul and hip hop.

New Words

album	/'ælbəm/	n. 相簿；唱片集；集邮簿；签名纪念册
appeal	/ə'pi:l/	n. 呼吁，请求；吸引力，感染力　vt. 对……上诉
ballad	/'bæləd/	n. 民歌；情歌；叙事诗歌
dominate	/'dɔmineit/	v. 控制；处于支配地位
genr	/'ʒɔŋrə/	n. 流派；体裁；种类
innovation	/ˌinəu'veiʃən/	n. 创新；改革
instrumentation	/ˌinstrumen'teiʃən/	n. 使用仪器；乐器法；仪表化
originate	/ə'ridʒəneit/	v. 起源，发起；发明
overview	/'əuvəvju:/	n. 综述；概观
portable	/'pɔ:təbl, 'pəu-/	adj. 手提的，便携式的；轻便的
region	/'ri:dʒən/	n. 地区；地域；领域
sentiment	/'sentimənt/	n. 感情，情绪；情操；观点；多愁善感
tailor	/'teilə/	v. 裁制；调整使适应
technique	/tek'ni:k/	n. 技巧，技术；手法
tempo	/'tempəu/	n. 速度，发展速度；拍子
utilize	/'ju:tilaiz/	vt. 利用
variation	/ˌvɛəri'eiʃən/	n. 变奏曲，变更；变种
video	/'vidiəu/	n. 视频；电视　adj. 视频的；录像的；电视的

Phrases & Expressions

appeal to	呼吁；上诉；对……有吸引力
gospel music	福音音乐（美国黑人的一种宗教音乐）
hip hop	嘻哈文化
pick up	获得
vocal harmony	人声合唱

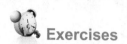

Exercises

Reading Comprehension

Choose the best answer to each of the following questions.

1. What is the passage mainly about?

   A. Different forms of pop music.

   B. Development of new music styles.

   C. History of American music.

   D. History of pop music.

2. What does "which" (Line 5, Para. 1) refer to?

   A. Pop music.

   B. Rock and roll style.

   C. The youth market.

   D. Recorded music.

3. Which of the following is NOT true about pop music?

   A. It is often performed in the forms of songs.

   B. It has changed into a number of new styles.

   C. It is associated with other forms of music.

   D. It originated in America in the mid-1980s.

4. How did modern inventions influence pop music from the 1950s?

   A. It changed the way people played and listened to music.

   B. It helped people understand American history and culture.

   C. It enabled other nations to develop their own style of music.

   D. It allowed performers to freely express their feelings.

5. What does the last paragraph imply?

   A. Pop music has developed into different types.

   B. Pop music has been dominated by American music industry.

   C. Pop music has been influenced by other types of music.

   D. Modern science has made pop music widely popular.

Grammar

分词(the Participle)

Pretest

Choose the best answer to each of the following questions.

1. _____ the weekend, the children are at home.

   A. Being   B. To be   C. It is   D. It being

2. All the factors _____ , his proposal is much valuable than yours.

   A. considering   B. considered   C. to consider   D. consider

3. _____ where she was from, she said she came from America.

   A. Asking   B. To be asked   C. Asked   D. When asking

4. _____ all my homework, I had a cold drink and went out.

   A. Finished   B. To finish   C. Finishing   D. Having finished

5. With his son _____ , the old man felt unhappy.

   A. to be disappointed   B. disappointing

   C. being disappointed   D. to disappoint

6. The old man closed his eyes, _____ with a smile on his face.

   A. satisfying   B. satisfied   C. to be satisfied   D. having satisfied

7. The chicken _____ at the moment smells good.

   A. to cook   B. to be cooked   C. being cooked   D. is being cooked

　　分词分为现在分词和过去分词两种。分词具有动词的一些特征，即具有时态和语态的变化，可以有自己的逻辑宾语。分词还具有形容词（可以做定语、表语、宾语补足语、主语补足语）和副词（做状语）的特征。

一、分词的时态和语态

　　过去分词只有一种形式（V + ed），表示被动意义或已完成了的动作或状态，没有时态和语态的变化。现在分词有时态和语态形式的变化，它有两种时态和语态，列表如下（以动词"do"为例）：

	主动语态	被动语态
一般式	(not) doing	(not) being done
完成式	(not) having done	(not) having been done

现在分词的一般式表示动作与主句谓语动词表示的动作同时发生。例如：

Hearing the good news, she jumped with joy. 听到这个好消息时，她高兴得跳起来。

（句中两个动作几乎同时发生）

现在分词的完成式表示的动作发生在主句谓语动词表示的动作之前，常用作状语。

Having finished her work, she went shopping. 工作完成后，她才去购物。

（finish 这个动作发生在 go 之前，也就是说是先完成了工作，购物这个动作才发生。）

二、分词的作用

1. 分词做定语

分词可以做前置或后置定语。

(1) 做前置定语：单个分词做定语通常放在它所修饰的名词前面，如：

a touching story 动人的故事 　　　 armed forces 武装部队

现在分词和动名词做定语的区别：现在分词表示名词的状态和特征，意思上接近一个定语从句；动名词表示名词的用途，如：

a sleeping boy 睡着的孩子（现在分词）a sleeping bag 睡袋（动名词）

a reading room 阅览室（动名词） 　　 a swimming pool 游泳池（动名词）

(2) 做后置定语：分词短语做定语都要放在所修饰的名词后面，相当于一个定语从句，如：

The goods (that were) imported from abroad are very popular. 从国外进口的商品很受欢迎。

The bridge (that is) being built now is three kilometers long. 正在建造的大桥长 3 公里。

2. 分词做补足语

(1) 做宾语补足语：能用分词做宾语补足语的动词不多，常见的有 see, hear, notice, look at, watch, find, smell, feel, catch, keep, set, have, make, leave, start 等。现在分词和过去分词做宾补的区别是：宾语与宾补逻辑上有主谓关系，用动词 -ing 表达，动宾关系用 being done 或 done 表达。如：

宾语　宾补（二者是主谓关系，表主动）

I heard her <u>singing in the next room</u>. 我听见她在隔壁唱歌。

He was glad to find his room <u>cleaned</u>. 他很高兴地发现房子已经打扫好了。

宾语　　　　　　　宾补（二者是动宾关系，表被动）

(2) 做介词宾语补足语：主要用在"with ＋名词（代词宾格）＋分词"结构中，分词做介词的宾语补足语，with 介词短语在句中做状语，如：

You can not leave home <u>with the child staying alone</u>. 你不能离家，而把孩子单独留下。

(3) 做主语补足语：分词做主语补足语多用在被动结构中，如：

The farmers were watched <u>working in the field</u>. 农夫们被监视着在田间劳动。

3. 分词做状语

(1) 分词可在句中做时间、原因、条件、让步、结果、方式或伴随情况等状语，分词的逻辑主语一般就是主句的主语。现在分词和过去分词做状语的区别是：分词与主句的主语逻辑上有主谓关系，用现在分词表达，动宾关系用过去分词表达。如：

分词　　（我们）听到──────　分词的逻辑主语 / 主句的主语
二者为主谓关系

Hearing the news (=When we heard the news), we jumped with joy.（时间状语）听到这个消息，我们高兴得跳起来。

分词　　给予（我们）──────　分词的逻辑主语 / 主句的主语
二者为动宾关系

Given (＝ If we are given) more time, we can finish it on time.（条件状语）给我们更多的时间，我们就会按时完成。

Not knowing (＝ Because he didn't know) how to solve the problem, he went to his teacher for help.（原因状语）不知道如何解决这个问题，他去求助于老师。

The mirror fell to the ground, broken to pieces.（结果状语）镜子掉到地上，摔成了碎片。

The students rushed out, shouting and jumping.（方式和伴随状语）
学生们叫喊着，跳跃着，冲了出去。

(2) **When/While etc. ＋ V-ing/V-ed** 结构做状语。 用于此结构的连词往往有 when, while, before, after, since, if, as if, (al)though, unless, as，这实际上是

一个省略了"主语 + be 的人称变化形式"的句子，省略的主语和主句的主语一致，如：

While reading (= While I was reading) his novel, I was absorbed into the story. 读他的小说时，我完全被里面的故事吸引了。

If / When (If / When it is) heated, water changes into steam. 经过加热，水就变成了水蒸气。

4. 分词做表语

做表语的区别：现在分词表示事物对人造成的影响，事物是主动的，常译成"令人……，使人……"；过去分词表示人对事物的看法产生的心理反应，人是被动的，常译作"感到……"。如：

The result is surprising. 结果让人意外。

We are surprised at the result. 我们对结果感到很意外。

这类词很多，如：boring, bored, interesting, interested, annoying, annoyed, frustrating, frustrated, astonishing, astonished, touching, touched, tiring, tired, inspiring, inspired, moving, moved, disappointing, disappointed, worrying, worried, encouraging, encouraged …

5. 分词的独立主格结构（Absolute Construction）

当分词做状语，其逻辑主语不再是主句的主语而是有自己独立的逻辑主语时叫独立主格结构，如：

The class being over(= After the class was over), he went straight home. 下课后，他径直回家了。

Practice

Identify *the present participle and the past participle* in the text? (The reference key can be found in this unit.)

Practical Writing and Reading

Poster

海报是主办单位向公众介绍和发布举行文化、娱乐、体育等活动的一种事务文书，通常写在大张纸上，张贴在公共场所。

海报具有醒目、快速和制作简易的特点，内容要真实准确，语言要生动而富于鼓动性，以便吸引群众。为便于阅读，篇幅要尽量短小精悍。有时可根据内容配上适当的图案或图画，以增强感染力。

海报的格式：

海报一般由标题、正文和落款三部分组成。

标题：可以直接在正中央写上"POSTER"，或者以活动的内容承担题目，如"AN EXCITING FOOTBALL MATCH"。

正文：这部分要写清楚活动的目的、意义、主要项目、时间、地点、参加的具体方法及一些必要的注意事项。

落款：要署上主办单位的名称和海报的发文日期。

以上格式是就海报整体而讲的。实际使用中，有些内容可以省略。

常见海报标题：

(1) POSTER

(2) GOOD NEWS

(3) FOOTBALL MATCH

(4) FILM SHOW

常见激发读者兴趣的句子：

(1) Please come and cheer for them.

(2) Don't miss it.

(3) All are warmly welcome.

(4) Catch the chance, or you will regret.

(5) Hurry up to…

常见正文所用句子：

(1) We will have a film show on August 5.

(2) There is a piece of news that …

(3) You can buy tickets from the students' union.

(4) The match will be held between …

Sample:

GOOD NEWS

A Chanukah Concert with

SHLOCK ROCK

Featuring:

Lenny Solomon

Tickets may be purchased at the Shul office.

General Admission Tickets: Seniors and Students

Time: Tuesday, December 7 at 7:30 p.m.

Place: Community Theatre

Sponsored by:

Fairfield County Jewish Organization

Task 1

根据下面题目要求，写一张海报。

（1）中秋节就要到了，学生会决定为远离家乡的老师和学生举办一场中秋节晚会，晚会上可赏月、吃月饼。

（2）时间：中秋节晚上 8:00—10:00。

（3）地点：学生活动中心。

Task 2

Directions: The following is a *poster*. After reading it, you are required to complete the outline below it (No. 1 through No. 5). You should write your answer briefly (in no more than 3 words).

All Senior Women

Including M.Div., M.A., Dual Degree, Th.M., and Ph.D.

All senior women are invited to a banquet.

Hosted by the Women's Center

Tuesday, July 13 at 12:30 p.m.

Mackay Campus Center Main Lounge

Come and celebrate your accomplishments with

A delicious lunch and fellowship with other!

We will also have the privilege of hearing from faculty and

students regarding women moving from seminary ministry.

Activity: A _____1_____

People invited: _____2_____

Hosted by: _____3_____

Time: July 13 at _____4_____

Place: _____5_____ main lounge

Come and celebrate your accomplishments.

Task 3

Directions: The following is a *sales poster*. After reading it, you should give brief answers to the 5 questions (No. 1 through No. 5). The answers (in no more than 3 words) should be written after the corresponding numbers.

GOOD NEWS

Winter Clearance Sales

All the goods are sold at fifty percent discount from March 1 to March 31. Please examine them carefully before you purchase. There will be no replacement or refunding. Hurry now for the best selection!

Personal Shopping Center

1. What is the poster about?

   The poster is about _____.

2. At what discount are all the goods sold?

   The goods are sold at _____ discount.

3. How long does the sales last?

   _____.

4. Can you replace or get refunded if you are not satisfied with the goods?

   _____.

5. Who wrote the poster?

   _____.

Task 4

Translate the following passage.

American pop music history has taught us important changes that occurred in the 1960s and 1970s, such as the development of a number of new styles, including heavy metal, soul and hip hop.

_____

_____

_____

Key to the grammar practice:

1. Country music even has its own theme park *called* "Opryland" where you can enjoy music shows and fun rides.

2. Jazz music, *developed* by African-Americans in the late 1800s, allows performers to freely express their emotions and musical skills.

3. Instead of just playing the melody, jazz musicians improvise different tunes *using* the same chords.

4. Rock concerts, *featuring* loud music and sometimes weird stage acts, have become a major part of the American youth culture.

期 中 考 试

创造性思维训练

请根据本教材中所学的词语、课文内容及其他知识，结合自己的专业确定题目进行创作。请用中文说明自己的构思。

Grading Criteria:

1. Creativity (30%)
2. Text-related knowledge that you have learnt from this book and richness (30%)
3. Topic relevance (30%)
4. Language expression (10%)

The Internet

Listening

Dialogue One   Netbook

Words and Expressions (I)

be used for			用来
incredible	/inˈkredəbl/	*adj.*	难以置信的
laptop computer			笔记本电脑
play with			玩弄
suppose	/səˈpəuz/	*v.*	猜想，以为
surf the Internet			网上冲浪
tablet computer			平板电脑
to an extent			在某种程度上

Patterns (I)

Learn the following sentence patterns to practice listening and speaking.

1. —**What's that gadget you are playing with?**

   —It's my latest toy—a netbook.

2. —Why is a computer called a book?

   —**I suppose it's because** there are lots of names for

different types of computers.

3. Does it mean **a netbook is used mostly for surfing the Internet**?

4. —**It's incredible how small computers are these days, isn't it**?

—It certainly is.

 **Exercise (I)**

This section is to test your ability to understand Dialogue One. There are five questions for Dialogue One. After the dialogue, you should decide on the correct answer from the four choices marked A, B, C and D given below.

1. What is Peter playing with?

    A. A notebook.   B. A laptop.   C. A netbook.   D. A desktop.

2. Which expression is NOT true according to Dialogue One?

    A. A netbook is a kind of computer.

    B. A netbook is a kind of book.

    C. Netbook is a mix of two words — Internet and notebook.

    D. Maybe there will be more tablet computers.

3. What does Peter mostly use a netbook for?

    A. Surfing the Internet and reading novels.

    B. Reading novels and checking emails.

    C. Surfing the Internet and playing games.

    D. Surfing the Internet and checking emails.

4. Which of the following is a name for the computer?

    A. Laptop.   B. Notebook.   C. Netbook.   D. All of the above.

5. What can you infer from Dialogue One?

    A. Computers will become smaller in the future.

    B. Computers will become larger in the future.

    C. Computers will not change in size in the future.

    D. Computers will have fewer functions in the future.

Dialogue Two   Online Shopping

Words and Expressions (II)

account number	账号
counterfeit goods	假货
have a try	尝试，试一试
It is...for sb. to do	
make purchase	购物
register at a website	网上注册
what's more	另外，而且
What's up?	出什么事了？
worry about	担心，担忧

Patterns (II)

Learn the following sentence patterns to practice listening and speaking.

1. —You mean shopping online?
   —Yeah. It's really convenient. It also saves time. **What's more**, the goods there are much cheaper and of a wider variety.

2. —**I'm** a little **worried about** security.
   —**It is easy for** thieves **to** steal my account number and password online.

3. —How do you go about doing so?
   —We need to **register at a trusted retailer website** and then follow their instructions for **making purchases**.

4. **There are different ways to pay**.

5. —**How long does it take for** delivery?
   —It usually takes 3 days within the city.

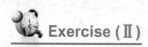
Exercise (Ⅱ)

Listen to Dialogue Two and complete it with what you hear.

Helen: You look upset, Li Mei. What's up?

Li Mei: My boyfriend's birthday is coming, and I've no idea what present to buy.

Helen: Why not search online? You can always find special birthday gifts from _____1_____.

Li Mei: You mean shopping online?

Helen: Yeah. It's really convenient. It also saves time. What's more, the goods there are much cheaper and of a wider variety.

Li Mei: But I'm a little worried about security. It is easy for thieves to steal my account number and password online. Aren't you worried about that?

Helen: Not really. I know that it happens, but if you _____2_____ reputable companies with secure websites, it should be ok.

Li Mei: What about counterfeit goods?

Helen: Well, some places sell them. So you have to _____3_____ where you shop.

Li Mei: I've never shopped online before. How do you go about doing so?

Helen: It's very simple. We need to register at a trusted retailer website and then follow their instructions for making purchases.

Li Mei: How do you pay?

Helen: There are different ways to pay: e-payment, COD, and _____4_____.

Li Mei: How long does it take for delivery?

Helen: It usually takes 3 days within the city.

Li Mei: Okay, maybe I'll _____5_____.

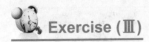 Exercise (Ⅲ)

Creative Thinking

Enjoy a part of the film *The Matrix* and discuss what you just watched.
You are required to act it out.

 Speaking

I Work in pairs: Make a dialogue.

Please choose one of the following pictures and then according to the
sentence patterns you have just learnt, make up a dialogue with your
partner. You are encouraged to use your rich imagination.

1

2

How the Internet brings us together

3

"On the Internert, nobody knows you're a dog."

4

Ⅱ Watch the videos and answer the following questions.

Video 1

🔍 Vocabulary ▼

arrogance	/'ærəgəns/	n.	傲慢；自大；自负
condescension	/ˌkɔndi'senʃən/	n.	屈尊；俯就
figure out			弄明白，理解
jealous	/'dʒeləs/	adj.	妒忌的，猜疑的
provoke	/prə'vəuk/	vt.	激起；惹怒；引起
remorse	/ri'mɔːs/	n.	懊悔，悔恨，自责
spite	/spait/	n.	恶意，怨恨
toss	/tɔs/	v.	翻动

**Questions**

What are they doing?

What does the man want to do?

Vocabulary ▼

bracelet	/ˈbreislit/	*n.*	手镯，臂镯
evil	/ˈiːvəl/	*adj.*	邪恶的，坏的，恶毒的
Goddess	/ˈgɔdis/		女神
hospitality	/ˌhɔspiˈtæləti/	*n.*	殷勤，好客
Istanbul	/istænˈbuːl/		伊斯坦布尔（土耳其西北部港市）
plain	/plein/	*adj.*	极普通的；平庸的

**Question**

What happened to her?

Vocabulary ▼

auction	/'ɔːkʃən/	*n.*	拍卖，拍卖方式
creep	/kriːp/	*n.*	讨厌鬼
isolate	/'aisəleit/	*vt.*	使隔离，使孤立，使脱离
original	/ə'ridʒinəl/	*adj.*	起初的；原来的
pirate	/'paiərit/	*n.*	剽窃，侵犯专利
porn	/pɔːn/	*n.*	色情文学，色情描写
purchase	/'pəːtʃəs/	*n. & v.*	购买
register	/'redʒistə/	*v.*	记录；登记；注册

Questions

What are they doing?

Do they succeed?

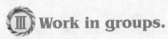 **Work in groups.**

Do you have net friends? Are you expecting to meet with him or her? Why or why not? Discuss with your partners, and choose a representative to report to the whole class.

That uncomfortable moment when Cyberdaters finally meet face to face.

> *Necessity is the mother of invention.*

Text

The Internet Transforms Modern Life

By Steve Almasy

In 1994, most people had to call the bank to check their balances. Or inquire in person, or wait for a paper statement to arrive in the mail. Baseball box scores were found in the newspaper. Weather forecasts came over the phone from the weather bureau, or on TV.

The World Wide Web has transformed the way people live, work and play. People can play travel agent and book all the elements of a vacation online. They can arrange for their bills to be paid automatically while they are gone. They can put a hold on mail delivery, find directions to tourist attractions and get a long-term weather forecast before they pack.

Even on vacation, they can log onto the Web to keep up with news from their hometown paper or TV station, and stay connected with friends and family. In its first decade, the Web altered the pace of popular culture.

Googling and blogging

Today, the audience for the Web numbers more than one billion and is growing.

The Web has added plenty of words to our lexicon, although some have yet to make the dictionary. If you had talked about Googling or blogging 10 years ago, you might have had a lot of listeners *scratching their heads*.

But like any youngster, the Web is growing. For all its uses, most people still go to the Internet primarily for e-mail. According to surveys, 69 million Americans sent e-mail each day in 2010, while 35 million used the Web to get news.

The Internet generation

The Web is changing the way people communicate, Daboll said. He pointed to the "Internet generation", teenagers who have grown as the Web has grown. One of their favorite tools is instant messaging, he said.

But the Internet isn't an orderly environment for the person who wants to pay bills, watch the latest music or take a virtual college class. It also can be a tempest. There are bad people out there — hackers and thieves.

But the Web can also help combat ID theft. An FTC booklet with tips to prevent or deal with ID theft is accessible on the department's Web site. The agency says it has received more than 1.8 million visits.

After all, 10 years ago, few people imagined it wouldn't be long before you'd be able to get a satellite picture of a city a continent away or read the local news from three time zones away or even order pizza without talking to the folks a few blocks away.

(424 words)

New Words

access	/'ækses/	n. 接近，进入
accessible	/ək'sesəbl/	adj. 易接近的；可进入的；可理解的
agency	/'eidʒənsi/	n. 代理，中介；代理处，经销处
agent	/'eidʒənt/	n. 代理人，代理商；药剂；特工
alter	/'ɔːltə/	vt. 改变，更改
automatically	/ˌɔːtə'mætikəli/	adv. 自动地；机械地；无意识地
booklet	/'buklit/	n. 小册子
bureau	/'bjuərəu/	n. 局，处；衣柜；办公桌
combat	/kəm'bæt/	vt. 反对；与……战斗 vi. 战斗；搏斗
hacker	/'hækə/	n. 电脑黑客
instant	/'instənt/	n. 瞬间 adj. 立即的
lexicon	/'leksikən/	n. 词典，辞典
primarily	/'praimərəli/	adv. mainly 主要地；首先；根本上
primary	/'praiməri/	adj. 主要的，首要的
scratch	/skrætʃ/	n. 抓痕，抓的声音，乱写 v. 搔痒，抓，抹掉
teenager	/'tiːneidʒə/	n. 十几岁的青少年

tempest	/'tempist/	*n.* 大风暴，暴风雨；骚动，风波
transform	/træns'fɔːm/	*vt.* 改变，使……变形；转换
virtual	/'vɜːtʃuəl/	*adj.* 实质上的，事实上的；虚拟的
youngster	/'jʌŋstə/	*n.* 年轻人；少年

Phrases & Expressions

it wouldn't be long before...	不久就……
keep up with the Joneses	比阔气；赶时髦（习语）
scratching their heads	绞尽脑汁
stay connected with	保持联系

Proper Nouns

| FTC | *abbr.* （美）联邦贸易委员会（Federal Trade Commission） |

Focus on

transform inquire agent agency alter instant primarily balance
accessible   keep up with   deal with

Study Independently

transform

1. We should try to **transform** heat into power.

2. How can internet media **transform** the society?

3. A little paint will **transform** this old car.

4. The magician **transformed** the girl into a tiger.

inquire

1. Let us **inquire** how to get there.

2. He is going to **inquire** about trains to London.

3. I'd like to **inquire** about the job for sales manager.

4. "Where's the station?" she **inquired** of a passer-by.
5. Several comrades dropped in to **inquire** about his health.
6. They are determined to **inquire** thoroughly into the matter.

agent

1. He is the sole **agent** for the airline. (agent for)
2. We should inform the insurance **agent** at the first time.
3. The secret **agent** tailed the spy.
4. Soap is a cleansing **agent**.

alter

1. Her face hadn't **altered** much over the years.
2. Beijing has **altered** beyond recognition (=changed very much).
3. He needs to **alter** his plan.
4. That event certainly **altered** the course of history.
5. Pollution can **alter** the ecology of an area.
6. Can you **alter** this suit for me?

instant

1. The film was an **instant** success.
2. He gave an **instant** answer to my question.
3. She made a cup of **instant** coffee.
4. He paused for an **instant**.
5. I'll be back in an **instant** (=immediately).
6. Fortunes can be made or lost in an **instant**.
7. I will meet you the **instant** you arrive.
8. The **instant** he got to the station, the train left.

 Practicing & Developing

Comprehension

I Choose the best answer to each of the following questions or complete the statements.

1. In 1994, people could get weather forecasts in the following ways EXCEPT
_____.

A. on the phone   B. on TV

C. on the Internet   D. in the newspaper

2. What do people do when they decide to go on vacation?

   A. They contact the travel agency.

   B. They pay their bills beforehand.

   C. They look for a tour guide.

   D. They make reservations online.

3. What does the phrase "scratching their heads" (Line 3, Para. 5) mean?

   A. Puzzled.   B. Amused.   C. Surprised.   D. Excited.

4. Which of the following is true according to the passage?

   A. Most people use the Internet mainly for news.

   B. A lot of people knew Googling or blogging 10 years ago.

   C. The Internet generation refers to those who use the Internet.

   D. The Internet has been changing beyond our expectations.

5. In what way does the Web change the way people communicate according to Daboll?

   A. Users can converse through instant messaging.

   B. The Web can help prevent and deal with ID theft.

   C. People can get a long-term weather forecast on paper or TV.

   D. Most people have to call the bank to check their balances.

Vocabulary and Structure

II Make the best choice to fill in each blank.

1. We can _____ electric energy into light energy as well as into heat energy.

   A. inquire   B. transform   C. combat   D. prevent

2. The police decided to _____ into the events leading up to the accident.

   A. inquire   B. transform   C. alter   D. investigate

3. When opportunity matures, we will appoint you our exclusive _____ for the USA.

   A. bureau   B. balance   C. instant   D. agent

4. You know, nowadays there are so many complaints about the shoddy

service of travel _____.

A. booklet   B. statement   C. agency   D. bureau

5. If your new coat is too large, a tailor can _____ it to fit you.

A. alter   B. design   C. inquire   D. order

6. The machine starts the _____ the button is pressed.

A. agency   B. instant   C. agent   D. lexicon

7. He is _____ concerned with his work, not his family.

A. orderly   B. automatically   C. primarily   D. eventually

8. It was not long _____ his name became a household word.

A. before   B. after   C. when   D. as

9. The government took these measures to _____ unemployment.

A. find out   B. put off   C. point to   D. deal with

10. The Browns bought a new car simply to _____ the Joneses.

A. catch up to   B. keep up with   C. look up to   D. end up with

Ⅲ Fill in each blank with the right form of the word given in the bracket.

1. I have no trouble _____ (get) used to a new environment.

2. The shipboard computer could _____ (automatic) alter course.

3. I'll arrange for my secretary _____ (meet) you at the airport tomorrow morning.

4. Medicine should not be kept where it is _____ (access) to children.

5. The flood victims were in _____ (instant) need of help.

6. She found the window open and something _____ (steal).

7. The advertising campaign is aimed _____ (primary) at young people.

8. The room needs _____ (clean) before the Spring Festival.

9. She will come to see you the moment she _____ (finish) her work.

10. If I _____ (leave) a little earlier, I would have caught the train.

Ⅳ Find the items equivalent to those given in Chinese in the table below.

A. agent bank   B. sales agent

C. trade balance   D. employment agency

E. real estate agency   F. intermediary agent

G. insurance agent   H. Xinhua News Agency

I. agency contract   J. favorable balance

K. preservative agent   L. credit balance

M. adverse balance   N. sole agent

O. intelligence agent   P. advertising agent

Q. agency agreement   R. cash balance

S. ecological balance   T. a general agent

U. secret agent   V. travel agency

Example: (M) 逆差　(P) 广告代理

1. ( ) 新华通讯社   ( ) 职业介绍所
2. ( ) 生态平衡   ( ) 保险公司
3. ( ) 销售代理商   ( ) 代理合同
4. ( ) 贸易差额   ( ) 房地产公司
5. ( ) 中介   ( ) 顺差

Ⅴ Choose the best translation.

1. We regret that the goods you inquire about are not available.

   A. 很遗憾，你们所咨询的货物现在无货。

   B. 很抱歉，你们所订购的货物现在缺货。

   C. 很遗憾，你们的货物并不令人满意。

   D. 我们很后悔没有及时向你们供货。

2. Unless you increase the turnover, we can hardly appoint you as our sole agent.

   A. 除非你们增加营业额，否则我们无法接受你们作为我方的独家代理。

   B. 除非你们增加营业额，否则我们无法指定你们作为我方的独家代理。

   C. 只要你们增加营业额，我们就同意你们作为我方的独家代理。

   D. 即便你们增加营业额，我们也无法指定你们作为我方的独家代理。

3. Success is primarily determined by making right choices, secondarily by making best effort.

   A. 只要正确选择，努力奋斗就能成功。

   B. 成功要靠正确的选择和艰苦的努力。

C. 成功的首要因素是奋斗；机遇是第二位的。

D. 成功的首要因素是选择；奋斗是第二位的。

4. The community college makes quality education affordable and accessible to the community.

A. 社区大学的优质教育得到了大家的欢迎。

B. 社区大学使得人人都有机会接受优质教育。

C. 社区大学使得高等教育得以在社会上普及。

D. 社区大学使得人人都有条件接受教育。

5. In industry, processing the information and designing the changes necessary to keep up with the market has meant the growing use of computers.

A. 在工业方面，处理信息和制订必要的改革计划以适应市场的需要意味着越来越多地使用计算机。

B. 在工业方面，处理信息和采取必要的改革以赶上市场的需要意味着越来越多地使用计算机。

C. 在工业方面，处理信息和改变设计以迎合市场的需要意味着越来越多地使用计算机。

D. 在工业方面，处理信息和按照市场的需要设计产品意味着越来越多地使用计算机。

Assignment

适 合 所 有 专 业

Topic: **The Future Internet**

According to the text, imagine the future Internet and demonstrate its application and help to your major.

Grading Criteria:

1. Rich imagination (30%)

2. Novelty (10%)

3. Topic relevance (40%)

4. Language expression (20%)

Reading

A Day in the Life of an Internet Entrepreneur

The purpose of this article is to give you a window into the lifestyle of an Internet business owner and in particular a *home-based* business entrepreneur. The example below is a typical day in my life. If you are presently considering starting your own Internet business I suggest you read the following:

I wake up at somewhere between 8 and 10 a.m. depending on what time I went to bed the previous night. I roll out of bed and switch on the computer which is in my room. Presently my laptop is my business so when I'm at home I either work in my room or at a desk in the dining room.

First I check and respond to emails and process jobs that have come through during the night from **BetterEdit.com**. Job processing means to assign editing jobs to staff members. I also manage ongoing projects including ensuring clients receive their jobs back on time, invoices are issued and payments are made. There are a lot of little things to coordinate but it doesn't take too much time and can be handled completely via email and through the Web.

In my room I have a whiteboard with a task list that I slowly work through as part of my working day after I finish responding to time sensitive emails. Generally I work on a website or do some form of writing for a blog / website or provide content for marketing materials. I also have to control other "standard" business tasks like hiring new staff, doing the bookkeeping and working with other businesses free lancers to get things done.

I spend a lot of time posting in forums and reading about Internet business. Occasionally I will have a Skype conversation with a friend over the Internet. This can be with one of my local friends or a contact from overseas. I don't feel this is a waste of time at all, as conversations with your peers can teach you a lot and stimulate new ideas.

I keep working until about lunch time, which is usually somewhere between 1 and 2 p.m. During lunch I will often watch a little TV or DVD. I love cooking and eating so this is one of my favourite parts of the day. I enjoy cooking for myself and often you will find me watching a DVD and eating some great food.

During the night I head back onto the computer and complete more web work and answer emails if any have come through during the day. I stay online until about midnight when I switch off and read myself to sleep. That concludes my day.

(452 words)

New Words

assign	/ə'sain/	*vt.* 分配；指派；赋值
bookkeeping	/'buk,ki:piŋ/	*n.* 记账，簿记
client	/'klaiənt/	*n.* 顾客，委托人
coordinate	/kəu'ɔ:dinit; kəu'ɔ:dineit/	*n.* 同等的人物 *v.* 协调，整合，综合
entrepreneur	/,ɔntrəprə'nə:/	*n.* 企业家
forum	/'fɔ:rəm/	*n.* 论坛，讨论会
freelancer	/'fri:la:nsə(r)/	*n.* 自由记者；自由作家
invoice	/'invɔis/	*n.* 发票，单据
issue	/'iʃju:, 'isju:/	*n.* 问题；发行物 *vt.* 发行，发布
laptop	/'læptɔp/	*n.* 笔记本电脑
previous	/'pri:vjəs/	*adj.* 以前的；早先的；过早的
sensitive	/'sensitiv/	*adj.* 敏感的；灵敏的；易受伤害的
staff	/sta:f, stæf/	*n.* 职员；参谋
stimulate	/'stimjuleit/	*v.* 刺激；鼓舞，激励

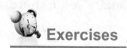

Exercises

Reading Comprehension

Complete the following statements.

1. From the passage we know that the writer does his job _____.
   A. by telephone
   B. in his office
   C. away from home
   D. through the Internet

2. The first thing he does in the morning is _____.
   A. posting in forums
   B. writing an article
   C. responding to emails
   D. chatting with friends

3. The writer spends a lot of time _____.
   A. coordinating small matters
   B. watching TV or DVD
   C. talking with friends over the Internet
   D. reading about Internet business

4. From the passage we learn that the life of a *home-based* business entrepreneur is _____.
   A. hard and stressful
   B. easy and enjoyable
   C. busy and tiring
   D. empty and dull

5. The passage is intended for those who _____.
   A. are successful in Internet business
   B. work as Internet entrepreneurs
   C. want to start their own Internet business
   D. enjoy working at home as freelancers

Grammar

虚拟语气 *(the Subjunctive Mood)* （Ⅰ）
——最基本的虚拟语气句型

Pretest

Choose the best answer to each of the following questions.

1. If my parents _____ here last weekend, they _____ me from going abroad.

   A. had been, would have prevented

   B. had been, would prevent

   C. were, would prevent

   D. were, would have prevent

2. If it _____ rain, the crops would grow better.

   A. should   B. will   C. is going to   D. was to

3. Many students think if there were no subjective mood, English _____ much easier.

   A. will be   B. would have been

   C. could have been   D. would be

4. If Mary had worked harder, she _____.

   A. would succeed   B. had succeeded

   C. would have succeeded   D. should succeed

5. The food _____ if you had been more careful.

   A. would not be spoiling   B. would not have been spoiled

   C. would not spoil   D. would not spoiled

6. If it _____ for the bad weather, we _____ the mountain yesterday.

   A. were not; could have climbed   B. were not; could climb

   C. had not been; could climb   D. had not been; could have climbed

7. If Tom _____ earlier, he _____ the bad food.

   Luckily, he was sent to the hospital in time.

   A. was warned; would not take

B. had been warned; would not have taken

C. would be warned; had not taken

D. would have been warned; had not taken

8. _____ him before, he wouldn't have made such a serious mistake.

A. Did I persuade   B. If I persuade

C. If I should persuade   D. Had I persuaded

    英语的动词一般可带有三种不同的语气：陈述语气、祈使语气和虚拟语气。不同的语气用动词的不同形式来表示。虚拟语气是一种特殊的动词形式，用来表示说话人所说的话并不是事实，而是一种假设、怀疑或推测（在条件从句中或让步状语从句中）；也可以表示说话人的愿望、要求、命令、建议等（在宾语从句、表语从句、同位语从句中）。使用虚拟语气，首先判断是真实条件句还是非真实条件句，只有在非真实条件句中才使用虚拟语气。通常有三种情况：①与过去事实相反；②与现在事实相反；③与将来事实相反。

一、最基本的虚拟语气句型：

	虚拟条件句中 谓语动词的形式	主句中 谓语动词的形式
与现在事实 相反的假设	If+ 主语 + 动词的过去式 （动词 be 用 were）	主语 +should/would/might/ could +动词原形
与过去 相反的假设	If+ 主语 +had + 过去分词	主语+ should/would/might/ could + have done
与将来 相反的假设	1. If+ 主语 + 动词过去式 2. If+ 主语 +were to+ 动词原形 3. If+ 主语 +should + 动词原形	主语+ should/would/might/ could +动词原形

1. 与现在事实相反：

    If I had time, I would attend the conference. 如果有时间，我会参加这个会议。

2. 与过去事实相反：

If I had known your telephone number, I would have telephoned you. 如果我知道你的电话号码，就给你打电话了。

3. 与将来事实相反：

If it should/were to rain tomorrow, we would cancel the match. 如果明天下雨，我们会取消比赛。

二、使用虚拟条件句要注意的两点：

1. 当条件状语从句表示的行为和主句表示的行为所发生的时间不一致时，被称为错综时间条件句，从句和主句中动词的形式要根据所表示的时间做出相应的调整。例如：

If you had taken my advice, you would recover now.

如果你采取了我的建议（对过去事实的假设），你现在就康复了（对现在事实的假设）。

2. 在条件句中，如果助动词是 were, had 或 should，可省略 if，把 were, had 或 should 提到句首，变为倒装句式。

If I were at school again, I would do my best.

—Were I at school again, I would do my best.

If John had arrived earlier, he would have met his girlfriend.

—Had John arrived earlier, he would have met his girlfriend.

If it should rain tomorrow, we would not go fishing.

—Should it rain tomorrow, we would not go fishing.

Practice

Identify the *subjunctive mood* in the text. (The reference key can be found in this unit.)

Practical Writing and Reading

E-mail

电子邮件方便快捷，在现代商务活动和人们日常生活中起着重要作用。电子邮件要格式正确，叙述准确，内容完整，用语简洁、礼貌。有时为了节约时间，邮件中可使用缩略语，如 Pls 表示 please, Qty 表示 quantity, U 表示 you 等。

电子邮件的格式：

From: 写信人电子邮件地址。

To: 收信人电子邮件地址。若有多个收信人，用逗号隔开。

CC: 抄送收信人。

BCC: 密送收信人。

Subject: 主题。适当的主题能够让收件人在阅读该邮件之前注意到它的重要性。所以，主题应体现主旨，意思明确、引人注目。

Enclosure/Enc.: 附件。

邮件内容部分与书信的格式基本相同，主要包括：称呼语（salutation）、正文（body）、结束语（complimentary close）、签名（signature）。商务邮件签名部分一般包括写信人全名、写信人职务及所属部门、地址、电话号码、传真等。

常见主题句子：

(1) Confirm your attendance of the meeting on Wednesday!

(2) Thank you for the job offer!

(3) Tomorrow's schedule

(4) Apology for poor quality

常见开头句子：

(1) How is the project going on?

(2) The greeting that you sent to Li Ming on August 10, 2010 has been picked up.

(3) I am writing to ask you to make a homepage for my company.

(4) This letter is about …

常见结尾句子：

(1) If you have any question or concern, don't hesitate to let me know.

(2) Your prompt reply will be appreciated.

(3) Look forward to your feedbacks and suggestions soon.

(4) Thank you and look forward to having your opinion on the estimation and schedule.

(5) Your comments and suggestions are welcome.

Sample:

From: john@abccompany.com

To: white@xyzcompany.com

CC:

BCC:

Subject: About the series meetings in the coming months

Dear Mr. White,

　　This letter is further to our meeting of last week at which we agreed to hold a series of meetings over the next two months on the implementation of the Customer Relationship Management Program.

　　As agreed, the meetings will be held every Friday from 9:00 a.m. until 11:00 a.m., and the location will be No.1 meeting Room, the first one to be held on August 20, 2010. Fred Johnson of your group is to act as the meeting coordinator and recording secretary throughout the process.

　　As discussed, at the end of the process, Linda will draft a summary report for review. As you requested, a copy of her c.v. has been enclosed.

　　I believe I have covered all the points that we discussed. If you have any question or would like to add anything, please give me a call at 82345678.

　　We look forward to seeing you at the August 20th meeting.

Sincerely yours,

John

Project Manager

ABC Company, Beijing

Practice

Task 1

根据下面题目要求，写一封电子邮件。

（1）你是兴盛酒店的一名员工。昨天有一客人向你咨询问题时，你的态度不够友好，顾客向经理投诉。就此写一份电子邮件，向客人道歉，希望客人能够原谅。

（2）你的 e-mail 地址为：andrew@xingshenghotel.com；客人的 e-mail 地址为 bettywish@store.com。

Task 2

Directions: The following is a ***complaint e-mail***. After reading it, you are required to complete the outline below it (No. 1 through No. 5). You should write your answer briefly (in no more than 3 words).

From: mary@marketing.com
To: feedback@lihotel.com
CC:
BCC:
Subject: Complaint about receiving poor service

To whom it may concern,

My name is Mary Harbinson and I frequently travel throughout the year as I am a sales representative. But last time when I stayed at your hotel, I was highly disappointed and unsure if I would ever stay at your hotel again.

During my stay, several rooms on my floor were extremely loud throughout the entire night. When I tried to complain to the Front Desk, I was told that there was nothing they could do about it. This nightly noise continued for 3 of the 5 days of my stay. While this in itself is intolerable, every day of my stay I had to go to the Front Desk and inquire why my room had not been cleaned during the day while I was out. Each day they told me that they were going to get to me soon.

The stay at your hotel was costly and it is unacceptable to be treated in this manner. I hope that this is a one-time experience that I will never have to endure again. Please respond with how you have handled this issue and how I can be sure this will never happen to me again.

Sincerely,

Mary Harbinson

Sender: _____1_____

Receiver's e-mail: _____2_____

Complaining about: _____3_____

The reasons for complaining:

    a. The front desk did nothing about _____4_____.

    b. The room had not been _____5_____ during the day.

The sender asks for response.

Task 3

Directions: The following is a ***resignation e-mail***. After reading it, you should give brief answers to the 5 questions (No. 1 through No. 5). The answers (in no more than 3 words) should be written after the corresponding numbers.

From: sun@engineering.com

To: tony@engineering.com

CC:

BCC:

Subject: Resignation of my position as Project Manager

Dear Mr. Tony,

    Please accept this letter as resignation of my position as Project Manager, effective September 30th, 2010. I am offering two weeks' notice—this will give you an opportunity to find a suitable replacement. If you would like, I am more than willing to provide training and orientation to the newcomer.

    My decision to resign was finalized after long and careful consideration of all factors. I regret leaving friends here; however, I feel the change will be beneficial to my long-term career goals and objectives. I assure you that I will complete any outstanding projects and business affairs before my departure— the transition will be handled professionally to ensure no internal or external problem.

    Again, it has been a pleasurable learning experience working as part of your team and I wish nothing but success for Chemical Engineering Ltd.

Sincerely,

Sun

Project Manager

Chemical Engineering Ltd.

1. From what position did the sender resign?

   The position as _____.

2. Why did the sender offer two weeks' notice?

   This would give the company an opportunity to find a _____.

3. Why did the sender resign?

   The change would be _____ to his long-term career goals and objectives.

4. What did the sender promise to do before his departure?

   He will complete any outstanding projects and _____ before his departure.

5. What was the sender's wish for the company?

   He wished _____ for the company.

Task 4

Translate the following passage.

Generally I work on a website or do some form of writing for a blog/website or provide content for marketing materials. I also have to control the other "standard" business tasks like hiring new staff, doing the bookkeeping and working with other business/freelancers to get things done.

_____

_____

_____

Key to the grammar practice:

If you **had talked** about Googling or blogging 10 years ago, you **might have had** a lot of listeners scratching their heads.

Creative Thinking

Listening

Dialogue One   UFO

Words and Expressions (I)

alien	/'eiljən/	*n.*	外星人
believe in			相信
contact	/kən'tækt/	*v.*	联系；联络
doctor up			掺假，篡改
if only			要是……多好
outer space			太空，外层空间
space shuttle			航天飞机
the National Holiday			国庆节

Patterns (I)

Learn the following sentence patterns to practice listening and speaking.

1. —**If only we could** travel to another planet for vacation.

   —Yeah, I hope so.

2. —**Do you believe in UFOs?**

—Sure. A UFO is just a space vehicle from another planet.

3. —**Have you seen** photos of UFOs?

—Yes, but they've all looked **doctored up.**

4. —**Do you think that** there's life on other planets?

—Yes, I think there must be.

5. —**Do you mean** we'll get to meet an alien from outer space one day?

—Yes, very likely.

 Exercise (I)

This section is to test your ability to understand Dialogue One. There are five questions for Dialogue One. After the dialogue, you should decide on the correct answer from the four choices marked A, B, C and D given below.

1. Why doesn't Li Ming have travel plans for the National Holliday?

   A. Because he has other plans for the holiday.

   B. Because he thinks it's too crowded everywhere.

   C. Because he doesn't want to go anywhere.

   D. Because he has an appointment with Edward.

2. Which expression about UFO is right according to Dialogue One?

   A. It is a space vehicle from another planet.

   B. It really exists in the real world.

   C. No one has taken a photo of UFO.

   D. All the photos of UFOs are doctored up.

3. What can be called UFO according to Li Ming?

   A. Any vehicle.　　　　　　B. Flying object.

   C. Air plane.　　　　　　　D. Space shuttle.

4. Is there life on other planets according to Dialogue One?

   A. Yes.　　　　　　　　　B. No.

   C. Probably.　　　　　　　D. Not mentioned.

5. Why are countries working hard to find a planet that people can live on?

    A. To make the earth less crowded.

    B. To find more natural resources.

    C. To find a place for vacation.

    D. To meet an alien from outer space.

Dialogue Two   Matching Name to Face

Words and Expressions (Ⅱ)

a good match to	和……适合
ask sb. to	让某人做……
conduct experiment	做实验
for instance	例如
go with	跟……相配
have sth. to do with	和……有关
How come…?	怎么会……?
look like	看起来像

Patterns (Ⅱ)

Learn the following sentence patterns to practice listening and speaking.

1. **—I'm always forgetting his name.**

    —It's really easy for me to remember some names, but others **take a lot of work**.

2. **How can Matt's face not go with his name? They're both his!**

3. **—What does it have to do with remembering?**

    —They were able to learn a name much more quickly when the names "fit" their expectations.

4. **It is easier to** remember someone's name if it's **a good match to** their face?

5. **—How come** you remembered Matt's name so easily?

    —Oh, him. He's my brother.

Exercise (II)

Listen to Dialogue Two and complete it with what you hear.

Yael: Hey Don, see that guy over there? I'm always forgetting his name!

Don: Oh, you mean Matt?

Yael: Yeah, that's it! You know, it's really easy for me to remember some names, but others take a lot of work.

Don: Don't feel bad. It might be because Matt's face doesn't ____1____ his name.

Yael: What? How can Matt's face not go with his name? They're both his!

Don: Well, psychologists at Miami University of Ohio conducted experiments showing a correlation between specific ____2____ and names. In one experiment, the researchers randomly presented participants with a name like Bob, Joe, or Dan, and then asked them to use computer software to draw a picture of someone likely to have this name.

Yael: And?

Don: The pictures had some striking similarities that ____3____ the name. For instance, the name "Bob" led most people to draw someone with ____4____, while the name "Tim" triggered more sketches with longer, thinner features.

Yael: But what does it have to do with remembering?

Don: In another experiment, the participants were shown ____5____ photos labeled with names. They were able to learn a name much more quickly when the names "fit" their expectations of what a "Bob" or a "Tim" should look like.

Yael: Is it easier to remember someone's name if it's a good match to their face?

Don: Exactly.

Yael: So, how come you remembered Matt's name?

Don: Oh, him. He's my brother.

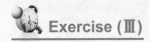 Exercise (Ⅲ)

Creative Thinking

Enjoy a part of the film *The Kid.* Please go on to develop it with your partners and act it out.

 **Speaking**

(I) **Work in pairs: Make a dialogue.**

Please choose one of the following pictures and then according to the sentence patterns you have just learnt, make up a dialogue with your partner. You are encouraged to use your rich imagination.

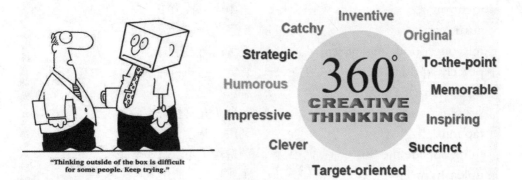

"Thinking outside of the box is difficult for some people. Keep trying."

Inventive
Catchy
Original
Strategic
To-the-point
Humorous
Memorable
Impressive
Inspiring
Clever
Succinct
Target-oriented

360°
CREATIVE THINKING

Vocabulary ▼

chancellor 名誉校长	lecturer 上课的老师
coordinator 协调员	Principal / President 校长
dean 系主任，院长	student / school counselor 辅导老师
Director of Studies 督学	support tutor 指导老师
faculty 教职员总称	tutor / mentor 导师

Questions

1. What are you majoring in? /What's your major?
2. What's the meaning of …? /What does … mean? /What does … stand for?

Ⅱ Watch the videos and try to complete the following tasks.

Vocabulary ▼

focus on		集中于；致力于
guru /'guruː/	n.	专家；权威；大师
misconception /ˌmɪskən'sepʃən/	n.	误解；错误观点
perceive /pə'siːv/	v.	感觉，感知；理解
perspective /pə'spektiv/	n.	看法，观点
sudoku	n.	数独（九宫格数字游戏）
tap into		利用，开发
think outside the box		创造性思考，打破常规
unleash /ˌʌn'liːʃ/	v.	释放

1. The creativity of … lies in …

2. It is (not) creative in that …

Task 1   Watch Video 1 and get to know the steps about how to improve your creativity.

	What is this step about?	**What will you do accordingly?**
Step 1		
Step 2		
Step 3		
Step 4		
Step 5		
Step 6		

Which side of the brain do the following activities relate to? Please list them in the blank boxes according to what you have heard.

imagination, colour, words, maps, shapes, analysis, lists, rhythm, lines, logic

the left brain   the right brain

_____   _____

_____   _____

_____   _____

_____   _____

the left and right brain

Task 2 Watch Videos 2 and 3 and tell your opinions on the creativity in the two ads.

What is Video 2 about?   What are the young man and the girl doing?

_____   _____

Task 3 Watch Video 3 and answer the following questions.

What is Video 3 about?

_____

What is the rat's creative way to get what it wants?

_____

Ⅲ Work in groups.

Have you ever had any creative idea? Give an example. What is it and how can you apply it? Discuss with your partners, and choose a representative to report to the whole class.

Imagination is more important than knowledge.

—Albert Einstein, American scientist

Text

Creative Justice

Throwing Criminals in jail is an ancient and widespread method of punishment; but is it a wise one? It does seem reasonable to keep wrongdoers in a place where they find fewer opportunities to hurt innocent people. The system has long been considered fair and sound. Yet the value of this form of justice is now being questioned by the judges. The reason, they say, is that prison doesn't do anyone any good.

Such considerations have caused a number of English and American judges to try other kinds of punishment for "light" criminals: all unpleasant enough to discourage the offenders from repeating their offenses, but safe for them because they are not exposed to dangerous company. They pay for their crime by helping their victims, financially or otherwise, or by doing unpaid labor for their community; they may have to work for the poor or the mentally ill, to clean the streets of their town, collect litter or plant trees, or to do some work for which they are qualified. Or perhaps they take a job and repay their victim out of their salary. This sort of punishment, called an alternative sentence, is applied only to nonviolent criminals who are not likely to be dangerous to the public, such as forgers, shoplifters, and drivers who have caused traffic accidents. Alternative sentences are considered particularly good for young offenders. The sentenced criminal has the right to refuse the new type of punishment if he prefers a prison term.

Since alternative sentences are not defined by law, it is up to the judges to find the punishment that fits the crime. They have shown remarkable imagination in applying what they call "creative justice".

A drunk driver was ordered to work in the emergency room of a hospital once a week for three years, so that he could see for himself the result of careless driving.

A thief who had stolen some equipment from a farmer had to raise a pig and a calf for his victim.

Graffiti artists have been made to scrub walls, benches. Other young offenders caught snatching old ladies' purses have been sentenced to paint or repair old people's houses or to work in mental hospitals.

Many judges think that alternative sentences may also be beneficial to the offenders themselves, by forcing them to see the effects of their crimes and the people who have suffered from them. It also provides some help to the victims. "*This*," says a "creative" judge, "*is true justice*."

(416 words)

Discussion:

1. A treasurer (会计，出纳员) has been found guilty of dishonest actions. What alternative sentences can you imagine for him/her?

2. A dentist was killed by a motorcyclist (骑摩托车的人) who was driving drunk. What alternative sentences can you imagine for him / her?

New Words

alternative	/ɔːl'təːnətiv/	*adj.* 供选择的；选择性的；交替的
beneficial	/ˌbeni'fiʃəl/	*adj.* helpful 有益的，有利的；可享利益的
benefit	/'benifit/	*n.* 利益，好处；救济金
		vt. 有益于，对……有益 *vi.* 受益，得益
community	/kə'mjuːniti/	*n.* 社区
crime	/kraim/	*n.* 罪行，犯罪；罪恶；犯罪活动
criminal	/'kriminəl/	*n.* 罪犯 *adj.* 犯罪的；刑事的；罪恶的
define	/di'fain/	*vt.* 定义；使明确；规定
emergency	/i'məːdʒənsi/	*n.* 紧急情况 *adj.* 紧急的；备用的
emergent	/i'məːdʒənt/	*adj.* 紧急的
forger	/'fɔːdʒə/	*n.* 铁匠；伪造者

graffiti	/grə'fi:ti/	n. 墙上乱写乱画的东西（graffito 的复数形式）
innocent	/'inəsənt/	adj. 无罪的；无辜的；无知的
jail	/dʒeil/	n. prison 监狱；监牢；拘留所 vt. 监禁；下狱
judge	/dʒʌdʒ/	vt. 判断；审判 n. 法官 vi. 审判；判决
justice	/'dʒʌstis/	n. 司法；正义
litter	/'litə/	n. rubbish, garbage 垃圾
offender	/ə'fendə/	n. 冒犯者；违法者；罪犯
offense	/ə'fens/	n. 犯罪，过错；触怒
scrub	/skrʌb/	vt. wipe 用力擦洗
sentence	/'sentəns/	n. 宣判，判决；句子，命题 vt. 判决，宣判
shoplifter	/'ʃɔp.liftə/	n. 商店扒手
snatch	/snætʃ/	vt. pull violently 夺得
victim	/'viktim/	n. 牺牲者；受害人；牺牲品
wrongdoer	/'rɔŋ'du:ə/	n. people who do wrong 做坏事的人；违法犯罪者

Phrases & Expressions

be up to	取决于……
be likely to	有可能……
emergency room	急救室
in jail	坐牢
not do anyone any good	对任何人都没什么好处
to see for himself	(idiom) to see with his own eyes

Focus on

sentence innocent judge emergent justice criminal offense
victim define be up to alternative beneficial

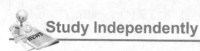
Study Independently

You are required to study independently the words and sentences given, and then you should talk about what you have learned and think over the usages in the text.

sentence

1. The teacher explained the difficult **sentences**.

2. The judge pronounced a **sentence** of death on the murderer.

3. He received a death **sentence**.

4. Cancer is no longer a death **sentence**.

5. The judge **sentenced** the thief to two years in prison.

judge

1. The powers of a **judge** are defined by law.

2. The panel of **judges** included several well-known writers.

3. Mr. Tailor is a good **judge** of the fine arts.

4. You should never **judge** a person by his looks.

5. **Judging** by his manner he must have enjoyed his meal.

6. Never **judge** a book by its cover.

innocent

1. Nobody would believe that I was **innocent**.

2. The court found him **innocent** and he was released.

3. He declared himself **innocent**.

4. They have imprisoned an **innocent** man.

define

1. Please listen carefully when I **define** your duties.

2. The boundary between the two nations is **defined** by treaty.

3. The police found a well-**defined** footprint outside the door.

4. I'll now try to **define** the term "popular culture".

5. Some words are hard to **define** because they have many different uses.

benefit

1. The new credit cards will be of great **benefit** to our customers.

2. I never had the **benefit** of a university education.

3. They are working together to **benefit** the whole community.

4. I'm sure you'll **benefit** greatly from the visit.

 Practicing & Developing

Comprehension

I Choose the best answer to each of the following questions.

1. According to the passage, what is the old type of punishment for law offenders?

   A. They are put in jail.

   B. They are made to do unpaid labor.

   C. They have to work in mental hospitals.

   D. They have to clean the streets of their town.

2. To whom is the alternative sentence applied?

   A. Bank robber.   B. Thief.

   C. Murderer.   D. Arsonist (纵火犯).

3. What alternative sentence is he likely to receive if a man is caught stealing in a supermarket?

   A. Taking care of patients in hospitals.

   B. Doing heavy work in the market.

   C. Repairing old people's houses.

   D. Scrubbing walls and benches.

4. Which of the following statements is true according to the passage?

   A. Alternative sentences are good only for offenders.

   B. Alternative sentences can be applied to all criminals.

   C. The criminal has the right to choose the punishment he prefers.

   D. The judges decide the punishment that the criminals deserve.

5. What does the creative judge mean by saying "This is true justice" in the last paragraph?

   A. The offenders pay for their crime by helping their victims.

   B. Alternative sentences gave the offenders severe punishment.

   C. Alternative sentences are defined by law.

   D. It is reasonable to keep the offenders in jail.

Vocabulary and Structure

II Make the best choice to fill in each blank.

1. If found guilty, they will face a _____ of ten years in prison.

   A. judge   B. sentence   C. victim   D. offence

2. In the war, hundreds of _____ people were sent to the prison camp.

   A. beneficial   B. emergent   C. innocent   D. alternative

3. The members of the jury are the sole _____ of what the truth is in this case.

   A. judges   B. victims   C. benefits   D. crimes

4. In case of _____, break the glass and press the button.

   A. community   B. emergency   C. justice   D. punishment

5. The police must do all they can to bring criminals to _____.

   A. offense   B. sentence   C. method   D. justice

6. You have to be able to _____ the meaning of the word within context.

   A. define   B. suffer   C. offend   D. snatch

7. His family was the _____ of the earthquake in Tangshan.

   A. criminal   B. offender   C. victim   D. justice

8. The way was blocked, so we went by an _____ road.

   A. emergent   B. alternative   C. innocent   D. ancient

9. It is considered an _____ to check into a hotel under an assumed name.

   A. application   B. accident   C. offense   D. interview

10. Fresh air and nutritious food are _____ especially to the health of children.

    A. beneficial   B. emergent   C. innocent   D. alternative

Ⅲ Fill in each blank with the right form of the word given in the bracket.

1. Our hope is to establish mutually _____ (benefit) trading relations between us.
2. We must keep as cool as a cucumber in an _____ (emergent).
3. He had been _____ (sentence) to pay a fine of $100.
4. Being a first time _____ (offence), the man received a light sentence in the end.
5. The _____ (crime) admitted having stolen the motorcycle.
6. The mountain was sharply _____ (define) against the eastern sky.
7. It is up to the International Olympic Committee _____ (decide) which city is chosen to host the Olympics.
8. The local company is running down and is likely _____ (close) within three years.

Ⅳ Find the items equivalent to those given in Chinese in the table below.

A. justice bureau	B. alternative energy
C. emergency call	D. emergency relief
E. justice department	F. prison camp
G. criminal case	H. criminal law
I. emergency room	J. crime rate
K. criminal procedure	L. emergency equipment
M. emergency light	N. community centre
O. alternative fuel	P. emergent treatment
Q. prison guard	R. justice court
S. emergency exit	T. criminal psychology
U. prison term	V. alternative medicine

Example: (D) 紧急救济　(O) 可替代燃料

1. (　) 刑法		(　) 可替代能源
2. (　) 急诊室		(　) 犯罪率
3. (　) 刑期		(　) 法院
4. (　) 司法部门		(　) 急救处理
5. (　) 战俘营		(　) 紧急出口

 Ⅴ Choose the best translation.

1. Online classrooms are quickly becoming a popular alternative to traditional classroom settings.

   A. 网上课堂很快成为备受欢迎的学习方式，是传统课堂以外的又一选择。

   B. 网上课堂将很快成为一种当下非常流行的替代传统课堂的学习方式。

   C. 网上课堂很快成为一种非常流行的学习方式，将最终替代传统课堂。

   D. 网上课堂很快成为一种比传统课堂更受人们欢迎的学习方式。

2. At some colleges, the amount of work you will do is left entirely up to you.

   A. 在有些大学里，要做哪些工作完全由你自己来决定。

   B. 在有些大学里，你的工作完全由你自己来做。

   C. 在有些大学里，你的工作量完全由你自己来决定。

   D. 在有些大学里，你要完全靠你自己的努力去学习。

3. I have no idea about her visit except that she is likely to be away for several months.

   A. 我对她的出访一无所知，只知道她想要离开几个月。

   B. 我对她的出行一无所知，只知道她可能外出好几个月。

   C. 我对她一无所知，只知道她可能外出好几个月。

   D. 我对她一无所知，只知道她想要离开几个月。

4. Though you may consider him innocent, in the eyes of the law he is guilty of libel.

   A. 你也许认为他无罪，可是从法律的角度来看，他犯了诽谤罪。

   B. 你也许认为他是有罪的，可是从法律的角度来看，他是清白的。

   C. 不管你认为他是否清白，从法律的角度来看，他犯了诽谤罪。

   D. 无论你认为他是否清白，从法律的角度来看，他是无罪的。

5. When boundaries between countries are not clearly defined, there is usually trouble.

A. 国与国之间的争端未完全解决时，通常会有麻烦。

B. 国与国之间的关系没有明确时，通常会发生纠纷。

C. 国与国之间的矛盾没有完全化解时，往往会出现麻烦。

D. 国与国之间的边界未明确划定时，通常会发生纠纷。

Assignment

1. 适 合 所 有 专 业

Creative Training

　　Choose one of the following words and make up a story individually or in groups.

emergent, offender, innocent, benefit

Clues

1. Close your eyes and think for one minute.

2. Write down sentences or words related to the word of your choice.

3. Do not care whether the sentences or words are logical.

4. Use five of the sentences or words to make up a story.

Grading Criteria:

1. Rich imagination (30%)

2. Content relevance and richness (40%)

3. Novelty (10%)

4. Language expression (20%)

Sample 见《高职高专英语创造性思维训练集》，北京：中国人民大学出版社，
　　　　2010：p79

2. 适合广告专业

Advertisement Slogans

Write *slogans* for the two advertisements with *creative*, *brief* and *clear* language.

Picture One   Picture Two

Sample 见《高职高专英语创造性思维训练集》，北京：中国人民大学出版社，2010：p76

Reading

How to Develop Creativity?

As everybody knows, all people are divided into two categories, idea generators and executors. Then, who represents the first group with creative personalities? They are artists, designers, actors, musicians, writers, creators—all those who introduce innovations into our life.

Executors are seen as "laborers". They act on ideas created by idea generators.

They are seen as followers with little creative thinking. Unfortunately, there are more people of that type than creative ones.

There is a view, and I subscribe to it, which claims that left-handed people are likely to be creative while right-handed people are likely to be executors.

The left-handed people have a more active right brain than the right-handed people. So, what? Well, I tell you that the right-brain is responsible for our creative abilities, and the left-brain gives us logic and analytic abilities, those peculiarly important for executors, accountants.

I do not intend to explain why the right-brain occurs more developed than the left-brain and vice versa.

The point is what is to be done with these hemispheres? What should "slaves" of their labor undertake in this case?

There are people, who show both two sides of personality, such as zeal and diligence on the one hand, and creativity and artistic exploration on the other. They seem to have the right-brain and left-brain working equally well, but it's neither about inborn peculiarity nor about childhood acquisition—the hemispheres' activation occurred much later and with their active hand in it.

So, what did they do to activate their another brain hemisphere? Who knows! Ask me what they did not! For instance, there is a TV telecast Brain Games, offering really good exercises for developing creative abilities with various invention activities, including absurd ones, for well-known or unknown.

To activate the right brain of development creativity it is very helpful to exercise the left side of one's body. You may eat with your left hand, write with your left hand or leg, whatever you like.

There are several additional things that may block creativity. One of the basic reasons is blocking fear. That is why, in case you want to develop your own personal creativity and become a creator some day, you are supposed not only to play with your brains and to eat with your left hand, but also to overcome fear if you have any.

(389 words)

New Words

absurd	/əb'sə:d/	*n.* 荒诞；荒诞作品	*adj.* 荒谬的；可笑的
accountant	/ə'kauntənt/	*n.* 会计师；会计人员	
acquisition	/ˌækwi'ziʃən/	*n.* 获得物，获得	
activation	/ˌækti'veiʃən/	*n.* 激活；活化作用	
additional	/ə'diʃənəl/	*adj.* 附加的，额外的	
analytic	/ˌænə'litik/	*adj.* 分析的；解析的；善于分析的	
category	/'kætigəri/	*n.* 类别；分类	
creative	/kri'eitiv/	*adj.* 创造性的	
creativity	/ˌkriei'tiviti/	*n.* 创造力；创造性	
diligence	/'dilidʒəns/	*n.* 勤奋，勤勉	
executor	/'eksikju:tə/	*n.* 执行者；实施者	
hemisphere	/'hemiˌsfiə/	*n.* 半球	
inborn	/'inbɔ:n/	*adj.* 天生的；先天的	
innovation	/ˌinəu'veiʃən/	*n.* 创新，革新；新方法	
peculiar	/pi'kju:ljə/	*n.* 特权；特有财产	*adj.* 特殊的；独特的
peculiarity	/piˌkju:li'æriti/	*n.* 特性；特质；怪癖；奇特	
personality	/ˌpə:sə'næliti/	*n.* 个性；性格	
subscribe	/səb'skraib/	*vi.* 订阅；捐款；认购；赞成；签署	
undertake	/ˌʌndə'teik/	*vt.* 承担，保证；从事；同意；试图	
vice versa		反之亦然	
zeal	/zi:l/	*n.* 热情；热心；热诚	

Exercises

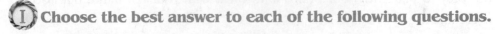

Reading Comprehension

I Choose the best answer to each of the following questions.

1. Who are creative personalities according to the passage?

    A. Judges.   B. Musicians.   C. Accountants.   D. Executors.

2. Who are generally regarded as executors?

A. Actors.　　　　B. Designers.　　　　C. Writers.　　　　D. Accountants.

3. Which of the following statements is true according to the passage?

A. The left-handed people are more intelligent than the right-handed people.

B. Some people are creators as well as executors.

C. There are more creative people than executors.

D. The right-handed people are creative personalities.

4. How do people activate their right brain?

A. Writing with the left hand.

B. Eating with the right hand.

C. Playing computer games.

D. Doing physical exercise.

5. Which of the following is NOT mentioned as a way to develop creative abilities?

A. Playing with your brain.

B. Eating with your left hand.

C. Performing a certain program.

D. Overcoming blocking fear.

Grammar

虚拟语气 (the Subjunctive Mood)（Ⅱ）
——虚拟语气在名词性从句中的运用

Pretest

Choose the best answer to each of the following questions.

1. It is important that a college student _____ English.

A. will master　　　B. masters　　　　C. master　　　　D. would master

2. It is strange that the girl _____ so rude.

A. is　　　　　　B. was　　　　　　C. were　　　　　D. should be

3. He gave orders that the experiment _____ today.

   A. be finished   B. will finish

   C. must be finished   D. was finished

4. He ordered that the medicine _____ three times a day.

   A. was taken   B. would be taken   C. should take   D. be taken

5. It is strongly recommended that teachers _____ computers to assist in their classroom teaching.

   A. to use   B. use   C. used   D. will use

6. His suggestion that you _____ ideas is reasonable.

   A. come up with   B. came up with

   C. must come up with   D. can come up with

7. The mother insisted that a doctor _____ immediately.

   A. has been sent for   B. be sent for

   C. will be sent for   D. sends for

一、虚拟语气在宾语从句中的运用：

用于表示命令、建议、要求等一类词后面的宾语从句中，从句的谓语动词用（should）＋动词原形。这类词常见的有：

order, command, suggest, advise, propose, recommend, require, request, demand, desire, insist 等。例如：

He suggested that we should put off the meeting. 他建议我们推迟会议。

二、虚拟语气在主语从句中的运用：

1. 在"It is ＋形容词＋ that..."句型中，that 所引导的主语从句中谓语动词均用动词原形或"should ＋动词原形"来表示虚拟语气，should 可省略。常用的这类形容词有：

important（重要的），necessary（必要的），essential（至关重要的），vital（极其重要的），natural（自然的），strange（奇怪的），better（较好的、更好的），urgent（紧迫的），incredible（难以置信的），advisable（适当的、可取的），crucial（关键的），appropriate（恰当的），desirable（合意的），imperative（迫切的）等。例如：

It's important that we (should) protect the environment. 重要的是我们要保护好环境。

It's necessary that we should take care of the flood victims. 我们有必要照顾好这些遭受洪水的灾民。

2. 在 "**It is** ＋分词＋ **that**…" 句型中，that 所引导的主语从句中谓语动词均用动词原形或 "should ＋动词原形" 来表示虚拟语气。常用的这类分词有：

decided（决定的）, determined（决定的）, commanded（命令的）, ordered（命令的）, suggested（建议的）, proposed（提议的）, recommended（推荐的）, arranged（安排的）, requested（要求的）, demanded（要求的）, required（要求的）, shocked（震惊的）等。例如：

It's demanded that we should come up with an idea to solve the problem. 我们受要求要想出办法来解决这个问题。

3. 在 "**It is** ＋名词＋ **that**…" 句型中，that 所引导的主语从句中谓语动词均用动词原形或 "should ＋动词原形" 来表示虚拟语气。这类名词有：

pity（可惜，憾事）, shame（遗憾）, no wonder（难怪，不奇怪）等。例如：

It's a pity that you (should) miss a good opportunity. 很遗憾，你失去了一次好机遇。

三、虚拟语气在表语从句和同位语从句的运用：

在 suggestion, proposal, order, plan, advice, idea, request 等名词后的表语和同位语从句中要用 "should ＋动词原形"，should 可以省略。例如：

My proposal is that we（should）hold another session to discuss the problem.（表语从句）我的提议是另召开一次会议来讨论这个问题。

My suggestion that we (should) take some difficult points into consideration has been accepted by others.（同位语从句）我提出的把难点考虑进去的建议也被其他人接受了。

Practice

Identify *the subjunctive mood* in the text. (The reference key can be found in this unit.)

Practical Writing and Reading

Memo

备忘录通常用于公司内部传递信息，将实情、信息、观察资料等进行传阅。备忘录的内容要客观真实，通常包括以下几个要素：谁，什么，何时，何地，为什么。行文应该简洁，要围绕主题来整理、提炼和概括，切忌记流水账。语言要有礼貌。备忘录不用致敬语，开头就叙述事实，结尾处也不需要结束语和签名。

备忘录的格式：

Memo: 标题，有时可以省略。

To: 收文人

From: 发文人

Date: 发文日期

Subject: 事由，只需名词或动名词几个词做简略陈述。

Message: 正文，直入主题、列出最重要的信息或结论。

Sample:

To: Erica Charles, Albert Gleak, Adrian Black, Peter Larmen
From: Linda White
Date: August 16, 2010
Subject: Casual Friday

As you all know, we have hoped to establish a casual Friday at the office for some time now. Because many of our superiors were unsure of the effect a casual Friday may cause on our clients, we have yet to receive the acceptance of an official Casual Friday. We have, however, received a hesitant acceptance of a "relaxed" Friday. For those of you who are not sure of the difference, here is what was explained to me:

A relaxed Friday means that we are able to wear business casual. This includes dress slacks, skirts, buttoned-up or Polo shirts and dress shoes. On relaxed Fridays, you are free to come to work without a tie or jacket. Pearls are not required. Some prohibited clothing includes anything resembling a Hawaiian shirt, sneakers or other athletic trainers or open-toe shoes or sandals.

As always, please discuss with me any question that you have prior to Friday. Please do not come to work challenging the boundaries of "relaxed" because you may endanger our tenuous agreement with our superiors. Thank you!

 Practice

Task 1

根据下面题目要求，写一篇关于公司修建健身中心（fitness center）的备忘录。

（1）健身中心修建工作马上开始而且两个月内完工。

（2）各部门选一名员工代表，与部门员工联系，征求关于活动和设备的意见。

（3）备忘录发给每名员工。

Task 2

Directions: The following is a *memo*. After reading it, you are required to complete the outline below it (No. 1 through No. 5). You should write your answer briefly (in no more than 3 words).

To: Custom Service Division, Sales Division

From: Helen Charles

Date: July 12, 2010

Subject: Copier Machine

It has come to my attention that many of you have difficulties operating the copier machine. Because of its constant paper jams and uneven ink output, the copier machine is a daily source of problems. We have read your numerous complaints and are happy to announce an exciting opportunity.

We recently contacted RHAM Copy Company about your concerns, and they have agreed to conduct a two-hour seminar all about the proper operation of a copier machine. This is a perfect opportunity for you to know exactly what to do if you encounter a paper jam or need to know how to operate properly. Food and beverages will be provided during this seminar. You will be encouraged to participate in the question-and-answer session as well.

The seminar is this Wednesday at 2:00 p.m. Be sure to stop by and ask any of your burning questions, and pick up a cupcake. See you there!

This memo is about: _____1_____

Problems caused by the copier machine:

   a. Constant paper jams

   b. _____2_____

RHAM Copy Company will conduct a _____3_____ about the proper operation of a copier machine.

_____4_____ will be provided during this seminar.

Please pick up a _____5_____ when you come to the seminar.

Task 3

Directions: The following is a *memo*. After reading it, you should give brief answers to the 5 questions (No. 1 through No. 5). The answers (in no more than 3 words) should be written after the corresponding numbers.

To: Department Heads

From: Betty Lynn

Date: December 11, 2009

Subject: Annual bonus leave

Starting January 1, we will introduce the following modification in our company policy with regard to annual leave: every year one employee from each department will be awarded special annual bonus leave for outstanding performance.

The eligible employees will have five additional days of annual leave credited on January 15. The bonus leave will be accounted for separately and will remain available until used, notwithstanding any other limitation of the total number of days of annual leave that may be carried forward.

We will have a meeting on December 15 at 9:00 a.m. to discuss the results of the 2009 performance evaluation and approve the final list of employees eligible for the bonus. The announcement to the employees will follow the meeting. If you have any question or comment, please let me know before the meeting.

1. What modification will the company make in its policy?

   The company will award special _____ for outstanding performance.

2. Will the total number of days of annual leave cover the five days of the annual bonus leave? _____.

3. Will the bonus leave be overdue? _____.

4. What will the company do to have a meeting?

   To discuss the results of the 2009 performance evaluation and approve the final list of employees _____ for the bonus.

5. What will follow the meeting?

   _____ to the employees will follow the meeting.

Task 4

Translate the following passage.

One of the basic reasons is blocking fear. That's why, in case you want to develop your own personal creativity and become a creator some day, you are supposed not only to play with your brains and to eat with your left hand, but also to overcome fear if you have any.

_____

Key to the grammar practice:

There is no subjunctive mood in this text.

Sports

Listening

Dialogue One   Becoming a Volunteer

Words and Expressions（Ⅰ）

apply for			申请
as long as			只要
by the way			附带问一句
check out			检查，核对
get involved in			参与
have to			必须，不得不
log in			登录
participate	/pɑːˈtisipeit/	v.	参加；参与
put in an application			提交申请
time consuming			耗费时间的

Patterns（Ⅰ）

Learn the following sentence patterns to practice listening and speaking.

1. —**Why** don't you volunteer for the Olympics?

   —Sure. / Good idea.

2. —**What do Olympic volunteers do?**

—There are eight kinds of volunteer categories.

3. —**I will apply for** this kind of volunteer.

—But being a volunteer can be tiring and **time consuming**.

4. —**By the way, when will I get the results after I put in the application?**

—You'll probably **have to** wait a bit.

5. —**Is there any possibility** that I'll get rejected?

—Um …

 Exercise (Ⅰ)

This section is to test your ability to understand Dialogue One. There are five questions for Dialogue One. After the dialogue, you should decide on the correct answer from the four choices marked A, B, C and D given below.

1. How can a student get involved in the Olympics?

   A. By becoming a volunteer.

   B. By checking out the poster at school.

   C. By logging in the official website.

   D. By quitting school.

2. Olympic volunteers can provide all the following services EXCEPT _____.

   A. quitting their jobs   B. liaison to VIP guests

   C. language services   D. urban services

3. Which expression about being a volunteer is true according to Dialogue One?

   A. Tiring.   B. Time consuming.

   C. Both A and B.   D. Neither A nor B.

4. Whose uncle is also an Olympic volunteer?

   A. Susan.   B. Liu Li.

   C. Phelps.   D. Not mentioned.

5. What can we infer from Dialogue One?

   A. Liu Li will see Phelps in the Beijing Olympics.

   B. Liu Li is very determined to become a volunteer.

C. Liu Li will get the results soon.

D. Liu Li will not get rejected at all.

Dialogue Two   The World Cup

Words and Expressions (Ⅱ)

at last		最终
beat	*v.*	打败
burn out		烧光，熄灭
can't wait to		等不及要……
cheer for		为……加油
dark horse		黑马
opening match		揭幕战
play against		同……比赛
root for		支持
the first round		第一轮

Patterns (Ⅱ)

Learn the following sentence patterns to practice listening and speaking.

1. —**Which team are you cheering for?**

or —**Which team do you root for?**

   —**I am a big fan of** Argentina.

2. —**What is your favorite team?**

   —My favorite team is the Netherlands.

3. —**I wonder if** those two teams **have ever played against each other during the World Cup.**

   —During the 1998 World Cup in France, Holland beat Korea 5-0 **in the first round**.

4. **I hope** Argentina **can hit the championship**, **'cause** I love Messi.

5. **It's really hard to forecast** which team can win at last.

Exercise (Ⅱ)

Listen to Dialogue Two and complete it with what you hear.

Mike: Hi, Diana.

Diana: Oh, hey, Mike. You look so excited.

Mike: You know what? The 2010 World Cup will begin tonight.

Diana: Yeah, I _____1_____ see the opening match.

Mike: The opening match will take place between the hosts, South Africa, and Mexico, one of the strongest teams in the Americas. Which team are you cheering for? / Which team do you root for?

Diana: _____2_____. I am a big fan of Argentina. What is your favorite team?

Mike: My favorite team is the Netherlands. However, I am very bullish on South Korea for this World Cup.

Diana: I wonder if those two teams have ever played against each other during the World Cup.

Mike: During the 1998 World Cup in France, Holland beat Korea 5-0 in the first round. Afterwards, the Korean team hired a Dutch _____3_____.

Diana: Is his name Hiddink?

Mike: Yes, he led Korea into the semifinals during the 2002 World Cup.

Diana: But I will still _____4_____ Argentina, and I hope Argentina can hit the championship, 'cause I love Messi.

Mike: Sure. Messi is a great guy. But you know, football is a team game. It's really hard to forecast which team can win at last.

Diana: Yeah, maybe there is going to be _____5_____.

Mike: Yes, so it is hard to say which team can get the world cup.

Diana: Well, we'll see. Time tells.

 Exercise (Ⅲ)

Creative Thinking

Enjoy a part of the film *Herbie: Fully Loaded* and discuss its result. You are required to act it out.

 Speaking

Ⅰ Work in pairs: Make a dialogue.

Please choose one of the following pictures, and then according to the sentence patterns you have just learnt, make up a dialogue with your partner. You are encouraged to use your rich imagination.

Vocabulary ▼

cartoon/comics /'kɔmiks/	*n.*	漫画
(direct) free kick		(直接) 任意球
score/make a goal		射门得分
skiing /'skiːiŋ/	*n.*	滑雪
slam duck		灌篮，扣篮
the extreme sports/the X-Games		极限运动

1. —**How often** do you play…?

  —**Twice a week.**

2. —**How long** have you been playing…?

  —**For three years.**

 Watch the videos and try to complete the following tasks.

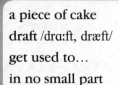

Vocabulary ▼

a piece of cake		小菜一碟，轻松的事
draft /drɑːft, dræft/	*n.*	（篮球）选秀；草稿；汇票；草图
get used to…		习惯于……
in no small part		在很大程度上

make one's debut		首次登场亮相
No problem/sweat		没问题，小事一桩
rookie /'ruki/	*n.*	新人，菜鸟
snapshot /'snæpʃɒt/	*n.*	快照，简单印象
take pride in …		以……自豪

Task 1　Watch Video 1 and tell your opinions on Yao Ming's role in NBA and in cultural exchanges.

Task 2 Watch Video 2 and tell whether it is "a piece of cake" to play some sports or do some exercises.

 Work in groups.

Nowadays, star athletes not only acquire big fame but also make good fortune. Do you think they really deserve both? Why or why not? Discuss with your partners, and choose a representative to report to the whole class.

> *Whatever is worth doing at all is worth doing well.*

Text

Something Interesting during 2010 World Cup

As Spain's triumphant players returned to joyous scenes in Madrid, the rest of the world was reflecting on a tournament which may have transformed South Africa but left some people with mixed feelings.

It is hard to believe now that for years there were doubts over South Africa's ability to organise this event. Fears about crime and security were largely *unfounded*. Whenever problems arose they were often overcome by helpful, smiling volunteers.

However, interesting things caught all people's eyes during the 2010 World Cup. Firstly, Paul the octopus was the biggest miracle in this world Cup. Before the final match, it had made a choice. The eight-legged sea creature had two boxes to choose from—one marked with a flag from the Netherlands and another with the flag of Spain—and it was the yellow and red banner it went for.

Secondly, there was "Vuvuzela". The tuneless plastic horn blown by fans was a top World Cup newsmaker. The origin of the word vuvuzela is uncertain. Some argue that it originates from the Zulu for "making a loud noise". Others maintain it relates to town slang for the word "shower" because it "showers people with music". More than 30,000 vuvuzela-blowing fans made a noise. But it will be best remembered for the South Africa's deafening trumpet.

Iniesta scores dramatic last-gasp winner

The most impressing match is the World Cup final. The Dutch tried to slow down Spain's passing game with rough, physical play. English referee Howard Webb, a former policeman, showed eight yellow cards to Dutch players, and Dutch defender John Heitenga was sent off the field during extra time. But Spain received its share of yellow cards—five. This match was described as "the dirtiest" World Cup final in history.

So what have we learned from this World Cup?

As with the Beijing Olympics two years ago, this felt like a nation's coming-out party, a chance to show off to the world. And it was a joy.

Brazil is up next in 2014. What the most interest things will we see?

(334 words)

New Words

argue	/ˈɑːgjuː/	v. 辩论，争论；证明；说服
banner	/ˈbænə/	n. 旗帜，横幅；标语

choice	/tʃɔis/	*n.* 选择；选择权；精选品
choose	/tʃuːz/	*vt.* 选择，决定
creature	/ˈkriːtʃə/	*n.* 动物，生物；人；创造物
deafening	/ˈdefəniŋ/	*adj.* 震耳欲聋的；极喧闹的
defender	/diˈfendə/	*n.* 防卫者，守卫者
dramatic	/drəˈmætik/	*adj.* 戏剧的；引人注目的
gasp	/gɑːsp, gæsp/	*n.* 喘气 *vt.* 气喘吁吁地说
horn	/hɔːn/	*n.* 喇叭
joyous	/ˈdʒɔiəs/	*adj.* 令人高兴的；充满欢乐的
maintain	/meinˈtein/	*vt.* 维持；继续；维修
miracle	/ˈmirəkl/	*n.* 奇迹，奇迹般的人或物
newsmaker	/ˈnjuːzˌmeikə/	*n.* 制造新闻的事件；新闻人物
octopus	/ˈɔktəpəs/	*n.* 章鱼
organise	/ˈɔːgənaiz/	*vt.* 组织
overcome	/ˌəuvəˈkʌm/	*v.* 战胜，克服
party	/ˈpɑːti/	*n.* 政党，党派；聚会
referee	/ˌrefəˈriː/	*n.* 裁判员；调解人；介绍人
reflect	/riˈflek/	*v.* 反射；表明；考虑
scene	/siːn/	*n.* 场景；现场，景色
security	/siˈkjuəriti/	*n.* 安全；保证
slang	/slæŋ/	*n.* 俚语；行话
tournament	/ˈtuənəmənt/	*n.* 锦标赛，联赛；比赛
triumphant	/traiˈʌmfənt/	*adj.* 成功的；得意洋洋的；狂欢的
trumpet	/ˈtrʌmpit/	*n.* 喇叭；喇叭声
tuneless	/ˈtjuːnlis/	*adj.* 不和谐的；不成调子的
unfounded	/ˈʌnˈfaundid/	*adj.* 无理由的；未建立的
volunteer	/ˌvɔlənˈtiə/	*n.* 志愿者；志愿兵

Phrases & Expressions

| as with | 正如 |
| be sent off the field | 被罚出场外 |

come out	出现，露面
extra time	【体育】加时赛
go for	攻击；尽力想求得
passing game	传切战术
send off	驱逐离场

Proper Nouns

Brazil	/brə'zil/	巴西（拉丁美洲国家）
Dutch	/dʌtʃ/	*adj.* 荷兰的；荷兰人的；荷兰语的　*n.* 荷兰人；荷兰语
Howard Webb		（英格兰裁判）霍华德·韦伯
Madrid	/mə'drid/	马德里（西班牙首都）
Netherlands	/'neðələndz/	荷兰
South Africa		南非
Spain	/spein/	西班牙
the World Cup		世界杯

Focus on

arise overcome dramatic miracle security organize go for
send off show off

Study Independently

You are required to study independently the words and sentences given, and then you should talk about what you have learned and think over the usages in the text.

arise

1. A crisis has **arisen** in the Foreign Affairs Office.
2. Difficulties will **arise** as we do the work.
3. Accidents **arise** from carelessness.

4. Great events **arise** out of small beginnings.

5. She **arose** from her chair when he entered the room.

6. They **arose** at sunrise to get an early start to the park.

overcome

1. You should **overcome** the difficulty.

2. We need to work together to **overcome** this enormous challenge.

3. We have **overcome** every objection and completed the mission on time.

4. He succeeded in his efforts to **overcome** these weaknesses.

5. He was **overcome** with sadness.

security

1. Terrorist activity is a threat to national **security**.

2. There are strict **security** checks on everyone entering the Opera House.

3. A large number of homes lack adequate **security** measures.

4. Parenting is about giving your child **security** and love.

5. The UN **Security** Council may impose economic sanctions.

miracle

1. It is a **miracle** that she survived the accident.

2. Do you believe in **miracles?**

3. Nothing but a **miracle** can save her now.

4. Maybe you should try yoga—it worked **miracles** for me.

5. A small but powerful word can make a big **miracle.**

6. Great Wall is a **miracle** of architecture.

dramatic

1. He enjoys the **dramatic** arts.

2. She made a **dramatic** speech at the meeting

3. *Jane Eyre* is a **dramatic** and entertaining version of the Charlotte Bronte classic.

4. The government is alarmed by the **dramatic** increase in violent crime.

5. In particular, economic performance took a **dramatic** turn for the better.

6. They got up a **dramatic** performance to entertain the foreign guests.

Practicing & Developing

Comprehension

I Answer the following questions or complete the statement.

1. What can we infer from the second paragraph?

   A. South Africa is capable of organizing the World Cup.

   B. There were no crimes committed during the World Cup.

   C. No problem has arisen during the 2010 World Cup.

   D. The World Cup was not as successful as people expected.

2. What does the word "unfounded" (Line 4, Para 2) probably mean?

   A. necessary   B. believable   C. worthwhile   D. baseless

3. Why is Octopus considered the biggest miracle in 2010 World Cup?

   A. It predicted five out of six games involving Germany correctly.

   B. It correctly predicted Spain's victory over the Netherlands in the final.

   C. It has not made a mistake when predicting the outcome of a football match.

   D. It predicted the Netherlands's victory over the Spain in the World Cup.

4. It can be inferred from Paragraph 5 that _____.

   A. the competition was extremely tough and fierce

   B. the referee was unable to control the situation

   C. the Spanish defender received a red card

   D. the referee issued five yellow cards to Dutch players

5. Which of the following is true according to the passage?

   A. There had never been doubts over South Africa's ability to host the World Cup.

   B. The word vuvuzela actually originates from the Zulu for "making a loud noise".

   C. The referee issued altogether 13 yellow cards and one red in the final match.

   D. Octopus chose the box marked with the flag of the Netherlands before the final.

Vocabulary and Structure

II Make the best choice to fill in each blank.

1. Should a serious crisis _____, the public would have to be informed.
   A. overcome   B. arise   C. maintain   D. transform

2. Please go upstairs and proceed through _____ check and immigration.
   A. referee   B. miracle   C. security   D. tournament

3. The biggest _____ in life is to find hope from hopelessness.
   A. miracle   B. security   C. benefit   D. treasure

4. Some people _____ that the death penalty benefits social security.
   A. organize   B. maintain   C. overcome   D. transform

5. They suggested measures to _____ current difficulties.
   A. arise   B. organize   C. maintain   D. overcome

6. Modern transportation has _____ the way we travel.
   A. transformed   B. maintained   C. overcome   D. reflected

7. Going to college brought about a(n) _____ transformation in her outlook.
   A. dramatic   B. triumphant   C. joyous   D. unfounded

8. My brother enjoys rock music while I really go _____ progressive jazz.
   A. with   B. for   C. over   D. after

9. He was _____ the field for his intentional hurting in the football match.
   A. ruled out   B. taken off   C. sent off   D. turned down

10. Mike has only driven to the pub to _____ his new car—he usually walks.
    A. take on   B. pick up   C. work on   D. show off

III Fill in each blank with the right form of the word given in the bracket.

1. Just call our Customer Care Hotline and ask a technician to help you make the right _____ (choose).

2. We are convinced that these differences can be _____ (overcome).

3. They always looked to him to settle the troubles that _____ (arise) among them.

4. After the _____ (defend) was in trouble, he just kicked the ball into touch.

5. ICAO stands for International Civil Aviation _____ (organize).

6. (work) _____ for three months, they finished a complicated design.

7. Many years ago, most people in China did not have the _____ (slight) idea of what Christmas was.

8. It is hard _____ (believe) that automobiles have come into common use within thirty years.

9. All you have to do _____ (be) to write your name and address here.

10. I wish you _____ (come) here last night. All of us were waiting for your arrival.

IV Find the items equivalent to those given in Chinese in the table below.

A. foul play	B. break through
C. send off	D. deceptive movement
E. penalty kick	F. slide tackle
G. penalty area	H. time wasting tactics
I. control the midfield	J. fair charge
K. close defense	L. cheering squad
M. blanket defense	N. free kick
O. fast break	P. corner area
Q. close-marking defense	R. turn a defender
S. extra period	T. goalkeeping
U. kick off	V. offside

Example: (F) 铲球   (V) 越位

1. ( ) 严重犯规	( ) 判罚出场
2. ( ) 合法冲撞	( ) 快速突破
3. ( ) 盯人防守	( ) 拖延战术
4. ( ) 比赛开始	( ) 带球过人
5. ( ) 罚球区	( ) 拉拉队

Choose the best translation.

1. With the development of science and technology and popularization of computer network, the network security has caused the high attention of computer users.

   A. 科学技术的发展、计算机网络的普及以及网络检察问题已经引起计算机用户的高度重视。

   B. 同科学技术的发展和计算机网络的普及一样，网络监督问题引起了计算机用户的高度关注。

   C. 随着科学技术的发展和计算机网络的普及，网络安全问题已经引起计算机用户的高度关注。

   D. 由于科学技术的发展和计算机网络的应用，网络管理问题已经引起计算机用户的高度重视。

2. All disputes arising out of the performance, or related to this agreement, should be settled amicably through negotiation.

   A. 凡因执行本协议所发生的或与本协议有关的一切争议，双方应通过友好协商解决。

   B. 在本协议的执行过程中所发生的与本协议有关的一切问题，双方应通过友好协商解决。

   C. 在本协议的操作过程中会出现一些争议，根据协议，双方应通过友好协商解决。

   D. 根据协议，凡因执行本协议所发生一切争议，都应由双方通过友好协商解决。

3. The real miracle of Dell Computer is not that the company started so well but that it has endured.

   A. 戴尔计算机公司的成功之处不在于它开始得非常好，而在于它能持久。

   B. 戴尔计算机公司的真实奇迹不在于它开始得非常好，而在于它能持久。

   C. 戴尔计算机公司的奥妙之处不仅在于它有良好的开端，而且在于它能坚持不懈。

   D. 戴尔计算机公司的真正魅力不仅在于它开始得非常好，而且在于它能经久不衰。

4. Whatever people think about them, they cannot deny the popularity of the minibook.

   A. 虽然人们对迷你型书籍有不同看法，它十分畅销却是不可否认的事实。

B. 无论人们怎样看待迷你型书籍，都无法阻止它的流行趋势。

C. 无论人们怎样看待迷你型书籍，都不能否认它是很方便实用的。

D. 无论人们怎样看待迷你型书籍，它十分畅销却是无可争辩的事实。

5. Landing on the moon is regarded as one of the most dramatic scientific adventures of the 20th century.

A. 登上月球被认为是 20 世纪中最激动人心的科学探索之一。

B. 登上月球被认为是 20 世纪中最引人注目的科学冒险之一。

C. 登上月球被认为是 20 世纪中最伟大的科学成就之一。

D. 登上月球被认为是 20 世纪中最难以置信的科学探险之一。

Reading

Difficult Adjustment

It only lasts a month but life without the FIFA World Cup will be a difficult adjustment for Chinese soccer fans, say psychologists.

A recent survey of 1,251 people by domestic research company Horizon found that 14 percent believed their health had been affected by the 2010 tournament in South Africa, which concluded when Spain defeated Holland 1-0 on Monday.

More than 70 percent of those polled also said they had suffered side effects due to regularly watching the late games, which kicked off at 10 p.m. and 2:30 a.m.

About 25 million Chinese fans on average tuned in for the games that kicked off at 2:30 a.m. each day, double the amount that watched the 2006 World Cup in Germany. In this case, side effects are to be expected, said health experts.

"I felt a sense of loss as soon as the World Cup ended," said Ling Guangxi, an engineer in Fuzhou, capital of Fujian province, on Monday.

Ling received a warning from his supervisor weeks ago after watching the late games left him exhausted.

However, 24-year-old IT technician Liu Huarui insisted that, although a die-hard Argentina fan, she had escaped any side effect of her monthlong soccer addiction.

"I did watch several games in the middle of the night but I quickly made an adjustment the next day," she said. "Yes, the World Cup is over. Yes, we miss it. But life goes on."

"They better eat some light food," she suggested, before explaining that for some fans, soccer is not a sport but a belief.

"Urban residents usually live under huge pressure. The World Cup is a way of (relieving)," she said.

(278 words)

New Words

addiction	/əˈdikʃən/	n. 上瘾，沉溺；癖嗜
adjustment	/əˈdʒʌstmənt/	n. 调整，调节；调节器
affect	/əˈfekt/	vt. 影响；假装
domestic	/dəˈmestik/	adj. 国内的；家庭的
exhausted	/igˈzɔːstid/	adj. 疲惫的；耗尽的
insist	/inˈsist/	vt. 坚持，强调 vi. 坚持，强调
monthlong	/ˈmʌnθˈlɔŋ/	adj. 整月的
poll	/pəul/	vt. 投票；剪短
pressure	/ˈpreʃə(r)/	n. 压力；压迫；压强
relieve	/riˈliːv/	vt. 解除，减轻
resident	/ˈrezidənt/	n. 居民
supervisor	/ˌsjuːpəˈvaizə/	n. 监督人，管理人；检查员
survey	/səˈvei/	n. 调查 vt. 调查；勘测
technician	/tekˈniʃən/	n. 技师，技术员；技巧纯熟的人
urban	/ˈəːbən/	adj. 城市的；住在都市的

Phrases & Expressions

due to	由于；应归于
kick off	中线开球
side effect	副作用
tune in	收听；调谐；使……协调

 Exercises

Reading Comprehension

Choose the best answer to each of the following questions.

1. The result of the survey showed that most people had _____.

    A. felt a sense of loss   B. suffered side effects

    C. had health problem   D. made a quick adjustment

2. Some fans suffered side-effects because _____.

    A. they often watched games late at night

    B. they kept watching games day and night

    C. they lived under huge pressure

    D. they had psychological problems

3. Ling received a warning from his supervisor because _____.

    A. he was late for work several times

    B. he made some mistakes in his work

    C. he watched football games during working hours

    D. he was too tired to work after watching night games

4. After the World Cup was over, Liu Huarui felt _____.

    A. she had a sense of loss   B. she was relieved of pressure

    C. she did not suffer side effects   D. she became addicted to soccer

5. The last two paragraphs tell us _____.

    A. why people live under pressure

    B. how urban residence live

C. how people cope with pressure

D. what the World Cup means to people

Grammar

虚拟语气 *(the Subjunctive Mood)*（Ⅲ）
——虚拟语气的其他特殊用法

Pretest

Choose the best answer to each of the following questions.

1. She is just a newcomer, but she acts as if she _____ my old friend.

   A. is   B. was   C. were   D. had been

2. I'd rather he _____ for Shanghai tomorrow afternoon.

   A. will leave   B. leaves   C. leaving   D. left

3. It's high time that the students _____ harder as the entrance examination is approaching.

   A. work   B. will work   C. worked   D. have to work

4. We have plenty of time and _____.

   A. mustn't have hurried   B. couldn't have hurried

   C. must not hurry   D. needn't have hurried

5. I went to see a film last night, but I wish I _____ so.

   A. didn't do   B. hadn't done   C. haven't done   D. couldn't do

6. Without computers, human life _____ quite different today.

   A. is   B. will be

   C. would have been   D. would be

7. Jenny _____ have kept her promise but to our disappointment, she changed her mind.

   A. must   B. should   C. need   D. would

8. We _____ last night, but we went to the concert instead.

   A. must have studied   B. might study

   C. should have studied   D. would study

虚拟语气还有几点特殊用法：

1. It is (high / about) time that... 定语从句中，用以表示"（此刻）该做……而没有做"，从句的谓语动词用过去式。例如：

It is (high) time she worked hard. 她该努力工作了。

2. If only 引导的感叹句（要是……该有多好啊）表示现在的情况，应用过去式；如果是过去的情况，应用过去完成式。例如：

If only I had followed Mother's advice. 我要是听取妈妈的建议就好了。

3. 由 wish 引起的表示愿望的虚拟语气

表示一种不可能实现的愿望。其谓语动词形式为：

表现在　过去时（be 动词用 were）

表过去　过去完成时

表将来　would, might, could ＋动词原形　　例如：

I wish (that) I were a superman. 我希望自己是个超人。

I wish (that) I had seen the touching film last time. 我真希望上次看了这部感人的电影。

I wish (that) I would/could go with him tomorrow. 我真希望明天和他一块走。

4. 在 "would (had) rather (would sooner, would as soon) + that 从句" 中，后面的从句用虚拟语气，表示一种尚未实现的愿望，其从句谓语动词用过去时或过去完成时。例如：

I would rather you told your mother the truth. 我希望你把事实告诉你妈妈。

I would rather you had gone there yesterday. 我希望你昨天就去了那里。

5. "as if (as though) 看起来……" 引导的从句中，常用虚拟形式。与现在事实相反，动词用过去时；与过去事实相反，动词用过去完成时；与将来事实相反，动词用 would（could，might）＋动词原形。例如：

She feels as if she were faint. （与现在事实相反的表语从句）她感到头晕。

She cried so sad as if her heart could be broken. （与将来事实相反的主语从句）她哭得很伤心，好像心都要碎了。

6. 不用 if 引导虚拟条件从句来表述，而用介词 **without，but for** 等引出的短语；并列连词如 **or，otherwise，but，though** 等引导的句子来表达虚拟语气。这时句中谓语动词仍采用类似 if 虚拟语气的相应形式。例如：

But for your advice，I would not accept his invitation. 要不是你的劝告，我是不会接受他的邀请的。

7. 情态动词 **+ have done**：表示对过去情况的推测或估计

(1) can / could have done： 表示"过去本来可以做某事，但实际上没有做"。例如：

As a clever girl, she could have passed the exam.

她是个聪明的女孩，本可以通过这次考试的。

(2) should / ought to have done：表示过去应该做而（实际）没有做的事情，含有责备或遗憾的语气，意为"本应该……"；其否定形式为"should not/ ought not to have + 过去分词"，表示某种行为不该发生但却发生了。例如：

The chairman should have arrived at 8:00 for the meeting, but he didn't show up.

主席本应该在 8 点到会，但却没到场。

(3) must have done：表示一种很有把握的推测，意为"过去一定做过某事"。例如：

It must have rained last night, for the ground is wet this morning.

昨天晚上一定是下雨了，因为今晨地面是潮湿的。

(4) may/might have done： 表示对过去情况的不太有把握的可能性推测，意为"过去可能 / 大概已做了某事"。例如：

She didn't get there before 6 p.m.   She may have missed the train.

她没能六点前到达那儿。她可能没赶上火车。

Practice

Identify *the subjunctive mood* in the text. (The reference key can be found in this unit.)

Practical Writing and Reading

Letters of Congratulations and Their Replies

祝贺信是对方有喜事向对方表示祝贺的信件。正文开头要写明祝贺对象和祝贺理由，中间可根据祝贺的事情表达自己的看法、建议等，最后再次表示祝愿。祝贺信要充满热情、喜悦，说些鼓励、褒扬的话，使对方确实感到温暖和振奋。赞美对方要做到实事求是、恰如其分，不要夸张，以免无法起到表示祝贺的目的。

祝贺信要整洁、大方，用词要恰当、简练，篇幅不宜过长。

常见开头句子：

(1) Congratulations on being awarded the Golden Prize.

(2) I extend my congratulations to you and your family on your graduation from high school.

(3) I take this opportunity to send my greetings and best wishes to you.

(4) I would like to sincerely congratulate you on your recent graduation from Beijing Union University.

常见正文句子：

(1) You did an excellent job convincing their management that Mary Green should be the agent to represent their new team.

(2) Graduation is the closing of one chapter and the beginning of an exciting new one.

(3) This post in the State Bank is one of the most highly prized posts both from the point of view of emoluments and the wide and quick opportunities for promotion.

常见结尾句子：

(1) I wish you greater success in your studies and research work.

(2) We wish you long days of bright sunshine.

(3) I look forward to seeing your continued success in dealing with this important new account.

(4) Best wishes for a successful event.

Sample:

June 12, 2010

Dear Bob,

Congratulations to you on your engagement!

You made a great and sweet decision. Miss Green is smart and beautiful. She is also very much well liked by all of us. You are lucky in getting such a nice and wonderful wife, and I should say, she is equally lucky to have you, a bright and handsome young man. You both are such special people that you deserve each other.

I am so happy that this great happiness has come to you. Please accept my heartiest congratulations on this happy occasion.

Wish you a lifetime of happiness.

Yours sincerely,

Sally Stevens

Reply to the above letter

June 15, 2010

Dear Mrs. Stevens,

Many thanks for your letter of congratulations on my engagement to Miss Green. You know Miss Green and I have known each other since childhood, and she has long been the girl of my admirations. After we both finished our master degree, I finally mustered myself to propose. Being pleasantly surprised, I got her positive response for engagement.

Thank you again for your good wishes and look forward to seeing you on my wedding day.

Sincerely yours,

Bob

Practice

Task 1

根据下面题目要求，写一封祝贺信。

在第 7 届英语口语比赛上取得了好成绩。假如你是 Viva Ghosh，给 Mr. Samimi 写一封信表示祝贺，并感谢他们，祝愿他们以后取得新的胜利。

Task 2

Directions: The following is a *letter of congratulations*. After reading it, you are required to complete the outline below it (No. 1 through No. 5). You should write your answer briefly (in no more than 3 words).

July 15, 2010

Dear Williams,

On behalf of everyone here at Western Towing Ltd., I would like to sincerely congratulate you on your recent graduation with high honors from Northeast State University with your Master degree in Financial Insurance.

Frankly speaking, we were not surprised to learn of your success. During the first time you did your practicum at our company, we noted how bright you were and how you had a very quick mind for business. Combining those attributes with your hard work and commitment to quality customer service, it is obvious that you have a wide-open future ahead of you. I can only hope that your experience working with us contributed in some way to your success.

On behalf of the management and staff at Western Towing Ltd., I wish you success in your future career and life endeavors.

Sincerely yours,
Mira Cajon
Sales Manager

The writer congratulates on Williams' _____1_____

Williams' major:_____2_____

Williams once practiced at _____3_____

The writer noted that Williams:

    a. not only is bright.

    b. but also has a very quick mind for _____4_____.

The writer wishes Williams success in his _____5_____ and life endeavors.

Task 3

Directions: The following is a *letter of congratuations*. After reading it, you should give brief answers to the 5 questions (No. 1 through No. 5). The answers (in no more than 3 words) should be written after the corresponding numbers.

Sept. 15, 2010

Dear Mr. Green,

    Please accept my heartiest congratulations on your recent promotion to the project manager position of Computer Engineering Company.

    I just heard the news today from Linda when she dropped into my office for her latest magazine. As you can imagine, Linda was very excited too!

    I know how hard you have been working to earn the recognition you presently enjoy at this company. I am sure your company has made a very wise choice. It's so nice when our hard work is justly rewarded. I am happy for you and you will excel in your new role as Project Manager.

    Please accept my best wishes for your success in your new position!

Sincerely,

Francis

1. What position was Mr. Green promoted to?

    _____.

2. Where does Mr. Green work?

   _____ .

3. Where did the writer get the news?

   _____ .

4. Why was Mr. Green promoted?

   He has been working hard to_____ .

5. What's the writer's wishes?

   He wishes Mr. Green success in his_____ .

Task 4

Translate the following passage.

A recent survey of 1,251 people by domestic research company Horizon found that 14 percent believed their health had been affected by the 2010 tournament in South Africa, which concluded when Spain defeated Holland 1-0 on Monday.

_____

_____

_____

Key to the grammar practice:

… the rest of the world was reflecting on a tournament which **may have transformed** South Africa…

期末考试

创造性思维训练

适合多专业

Imagine that you will be launched into space someday.

What will you plan to do? Why? Please describe your work on Space.

Grading Criteria:

1. With imagination (30%)

2. Content relevance and richness (30%)

3. Novelty and relation to your major (30%)

4. Language expression (10%)

Glossary

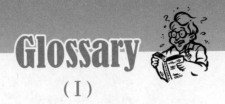

（Ⅰ）

Unit One

Text

astronaut /'æstrənɔːt/	*n.* 宇航员
bar /bɑː/	*n.* 酒吧；障碍　*vt.* ban 禁止
basically /'beisikəli/	*adv.* mainly 主要地，基本上
crew /kruː/	*n.* 队，组；全体人员，全体船员
disaster /ˌdi'zɑːstə/	*n.* 灾难，灾祸；不幸
Endeavour /in'devə/	"奋进"号航天飞机
equipment /i'kwipmənt/	*n.* device 设备，装备；器材
explode /ik'spləud/	*v.* 爆炸
launch /lɔːntʃ, lɑːntʃ/	*vt. & n.* 发射（导弹、火箭等）；发起
link /liŋk/	*n.* 链环，环节；联系，关系
mission /'miʃən/	*n.* task 使命，任务；delegation 代表团
orbit /'ɔːbit/	*n.* 轨道；眼眶
supply /sə'plai/	*n.* 物资；供应品；贮备量
substitute /'sʌbstitjuːt, -tuːt/	*n.* 代替者，替代品　*v.* 用……代替，代替
video /'vidiəu/	*n.* 视频　*adj.* 视频的；录像的；电视的
get to	到达；开始；着手处理；接触到
in case	万一；假使
relate with	使相关，使符合
space shuttle	航天飞机
space station	空间站，太空站
Boise /'bɔisi/	博伊西（美国爱达荷州首府）
Idaho /'aidəhəu/	美国爱达荷州
McCall	麦考尔（美国爱达荷州的一个城市）
NASA /'næsə, 'nei-/	*abbr.* 美国国家航空航天局（National Aeronautics and Space Administration）

Reading

affect /ə'fekt/	*vt.* 影响
calmly /'kɑːmli/	*adv.* 冷静地；平静地；安静地
circle /'səːkl/	*vt.* 环绕……移动
commander /kə'mɑːndə/	*n.* 指挥官
fix /fiks/	*vt.* 使固定；修理；安装
flier /'flaiə/	*n.* 飞行员；飞行物
lander /'lændə/	*n.* 着陆器
lightning /'laitniŋ/	*n.* 闪电
navy /'neivi/	*n.* 海军
orbit /'ɔːbit/	*v.* 绕轨道运行，旋转运动，转圈
path /pɑːθ, pæθ/	*n.* 小路；轨道
pilot /'pailət/	*n.* 飞行员；领航员
rescue /'reskjuː/	*vt.* 援救，救出，营救
scientific /saiən'tifik/	*adj.* 科学的
spacecraft /'speiskrɑːft, -kræft/	*n.* 宇宙飞船，航天器
command module	指挥舱；驾驶舱
lift off	（火箭等）发射；（直升机）起飞
remain in	待在屋里，不外出；保持处于（某种状态）
scientific instrument	科学仪器
unmanned spacecraft	无人驾驶飞机；无人宇宙飞船

Unit Two

Text

astonishing /ə'stɔniʃiŋ/	*adj.* 惊人的；令人惊讶的
demo /'deməu/	*n.* 演示；样本唱片
depth /depθ/	*n.* 深度；深奥
enhance /in'hɑːns, -hæns/	*vt.* 提高；加强；增加
establish /i'stæbliʃ/	*vt.* 建立；创办；安置
exist /ig'zist/	*vi.* 存在；生存；生活；继续存在
existence /ig'zistəns/	*n.* 存在；生存；生活；存在物
eyewear /'ai,wɛə/	*n.* 眼镜；眼镜防护；护目镜
feature /'fiːtʃə/	*n.* 特色，特征　*vt.* 特写；以……为特色

fuzzy /'fʌzi/	*adj.* 模糊的；失真的；有绒毛的
illusion /i'lju:ʒən/	*n.* 幻觉，错觉；错误的观念或信仰
kid	*n.* 儿童 *v.* 开玩笑
must	*n.* 必须的条件，不可缺少的东西
nonetheless /ˌnʌnðə'les/	*conj.* 尽管如此，但是
personality /ˌpə:sə'næləti/	*n.* 个性；品格；名人
projection /prəu'dʒekʃən/	*n.* 投射；规划；突出
resurgence /ri'sə:dʒəns/	*n.* 复活；再现；再起
stir /stə:/	*n.* 搅拌；轰动 *vt.* 搅拌；激起；惹起
stirring /'stə:riŋ/	*adj.* 激动人心的；活跃的
themed /θi:md/	*adj.* 以……为主题的
venue /'venju:/	*n.* 场地，场馆
be into…	对……很有兴趣，极喜欢；懂得
depend on	取决于；依赖于
end up	结束；死亡
even when	即使当
motion picture	电影
on earth	究竟
Avatar	电影《阿凡达》

Reading

awful /'ɔ:ful/	*adj.* 可怕的，庄严的
contender /kən'tendə/	*n.* 竞争者；争夺者
definitely /'definitli/	*adv.* 清楚地，当然；明确地，肯定地
depth /depθ/	*n.* 深度；深奥
dreamscape /'dri:mskeip/	*n.* 梦幻景象，幻景
enchanting /in'tʃɑ:ntiŋ, en-/	*adj.* 迷人的；妩媚的
expansion /ik'spænʃən/	*n.* 膨胀；阐述；扩张物
handful /'hændful/	*n.* 少数；一把；棘手事
hater /'heitə/	*n.* 怀恨者
heighten /'haitən/	*v.* 提高，升高
innocent /'inəsənt/	*n.* 天真的人；笨蛋

premise /'premis/	n. 前提；上述各项
smug /smʌg/	n. 书呆子；自命不凡的家伙
star /stɑː/	n. 星，明星　vt. 由……主演　vi. 担任主角
texture /'tekstʃə/	n. 质地；纹理；结构；本质，实质
underlying /ˌʌndə'laiiŋ/	adj. 潜在的；根本的；在下面的；优先的
zeal /ziːl/	n. 热情；热心；热诚
miss out	错过；遗漏；省略
pick up	捡起；获得；收拾
rank among	跻身于；属于之列

Unit Three

Text

address /ə'dres/	n. 地址；演讲　vt. 演说；从事
banjo /'bændʒəu/	n. 班卓琴
chant /tʃɑːnt, tʃænt/	n. 圣歌；赞美诗
characteristic /ˌkærəktə'ristik/	n. 特征；特性；特色
chord /kɔːd/	n. 弦；和弦
chorus /'kɔːrəs/	n. 合唱队；齐声　vt. 合唱
classical /'klæsikəl/	n. 古典音乐　adj. 古典的；经典的
down-to-earth /'dauntə'əːθ/	adj. 实际的；现实的
explosive /ik'spləusiv/	n. 炸药；爆炸物　adj. 爆炸的；爆炸性的
favorite /'feivərit/	adj. 最喜爱的；中意的；宠爱的
folk /fəuk/	n. 民族；亲属（复数）　adj. 民间的
hardship /'hɑːdʃip/	n. 困苦；苦难；艰难险阻
ignorant /'ignərənt/	adj. 无知的；愚昧的
ignore /ig'nɔː/	vt. 驳回诉讼；忽视；不理睬
improvise /'imprəvaiz/	vt. 即兴创作；即兴表演
melody /'melədi/	n. 旋律；歌曲；美妙的音乐
origin /'ɔridʒin, 'ɔː-/	n. 起源；原点；出身；开端
originate /ə'ridʒəneit/	vt. 引起；创作　vi. 发源；发生；起航
performer /pə'fɔːmə/	n. 执行者；演奏者

popular /'pɔpjulə/	*adj.* 流行的，通俗的；受欢迎的
rap /ræp/	*vt.* 抢走；轻敲 *vi.* 敲击；交谈 *n.* 说唱乐
rapper /'ræpə/	*n.* 说唱歌手
rebel /'rebəl, ri'bel/	*n.* 反叛者；叛徒 *vi.* 反叛；反抗
represent /ˌrepri'zent/	*vt.* 代表；表现；描绘 *vi.* 代表；提出异议
rhyming /'raimiŋ/	*n.* 押韵 *adj.* 押韵的
ride /raid/	*vt.* 骑；乘；控制
theme /θi:m/	*n.* 主题；主旋律；题目
weird /wiəd/	*adj.* 怪异的；不可思议的；超自然的
vulgar /'vʌlgə/	*adj.* 粗俗的；通俗的；本土的
bring back	拿回来；使……恢复；使……回忆起来
go on	继续；过去；继续下去；发生
grow up	成长，逐渐形成

Reading

album /'ælbəm/	*n.* 相簿；唱片集；集邮簿；签名纪念册
appeal /ə'pi:l/	*n.* 呼吁，请求；吸引力，感染力 *vt.* 对……上诉
ballad	*n.* 民歌；情歌；叙事诗歌
dominate /'dɔmineit/	*v.* 控制；处于支配地位
genr /'ʒɔŋrə/	*n.* 流派；体裁；种类
innovation /ˌinəu'veiʃən/	*n.* 创新；改革
instrumentation /ˌinstrumen'teiʃən/	*n.* 使用仪器；乐器法；仪表化
originate /ə'ridʒəneit/	*v.* 起源，发起；发明
overview /'əuvəvju:/	*n.* 综述；概观
portable /'pɔ:təbl, 'pəu-/	*adj.* 手提的，便携式的；轻便的
region	*n.* 地区；地域；领域
sentiment /'sentimənt/	*n.* 感情，情绪；情操；观点；多愁善感
tailor /'teilə/	*v.* 裁制；调整使适应
technique /tek'ni:k/	*n.* 技巧，技术；手法
tempo /'tempəu/	*n.* 速度，发展速度；拍子
utilize /'ju:tilaiz/	*vt.* 利用
variation /ˌvɛəri'eiʃən/	*n.* 变奏曲，变更；变种

video /'vɪdiəu/	*n.* 视频；电视　*adj.* 视频的；录像的；电视的
appeal to	呼吁；上诉；对……有吸引力
gospel music	福音音乐（美国黑人的一种宗教音乐）
hip hop	嘻哈文化
pick up	获得
vocal harmony	人声合唱

Unit Four

Text

access /'ækses/	*n.* 接近，进入
accessible /ək'sesəbl/	*adj.* 易接近的；可进入的；可理解的
agency /'eidʒənsi/	*n.* 代理，中介；代理处，经销处
agent /'eidʒənt/	*n.* 代理人，代理商；药剂；特工
alter /'ɔːltə/	*vt.* 改变，更改
automatically /ˌɔːtə'mætikəli/	*adv.* 自动地；机械地；无意识地
booklet /'buklit/	*n.* 小册子
bureau /'bjuərəu/	*n.* 局，处；衣柜；办公桌
combat /kəm'bæt/	*vt.* 反对；与……战斗　*vi.* 战斗；搏斗
hacker /'hækə/	*n.* 电脑黑客
instant /'instənt/	*n.* 瞬间　*adj.* 立即的
lexicon /'leksikən/	*n.* 词典，辞典
primarily /'praimərəli, prai'me-/	*adv.* mainly 主要地；首先；根本上
primary /'praiməri/	*adj.* 主要的，首要的
scratch /skrætʃ/	*n.* 抓痕，抓的声音，乱写　*v.* 搔痒，抓，抹掉
teenager /'tiːneidʒə/	*n.* 十几岁的青少年
tempest /'tempist/	*n.* 大风暴，暴风雨；骚动，风波
transform /træns'fɔːm/	*vt.* 改变，使……变形；转换
virtual /'vəːtʃuəl/	*adj.* 实质上的，事实上的；虚拟的
youngster /'jʌŋstə/	*n.* 年轻人；少年
it wouldn't be long before...	不久就……
keep up with the Joneses	比阔气；赶时髦（习语）

scratching their heads	绞尽脑汁
stay connected with	保持联系
FTC	*abbr.* （美）联邦贸易委员会（Federal Trade Commission）

Reading

assign /ə'sain/	*vt.* 分配；指派；赋值
bookkeeping /'buk.ki:piŋ/	*n.* 记账，簿记
client /'klaiənt/	*n.* 顾客，委托人
coordinate /kəu'ɔːdinit; kəu'ɔːdineit/	*n.* 同等的人物 *v.* 协调，整合，综合
entrepreneur /,ɔntrəprə'nə:/	*n.* 企业家
forum /'fɔːrəm/	*n.* 论坛，讨论会
freelancer /'fri:lɑːnsə(r)/	*n.* 自由记者；自由作家
invoice /'invɔis/	*n.* 发票，单据
issue /'iʃju:, 'isju:/	*n.* 问题；发行物 *vt.* 发行，发布
laptop /'læptɔp//	*n.* 笔记本电脑
previous /'pri:vjəs/	*adj.* 以前的；早先的；过早的
sensitive /'sensitiv/	*adj.* 敏感的；灵敏的；易受伤害的
staff /stɑːf, stæf/	*n.* 职员；参谋
stimulate /'stimjuleit/	*v.* 刺激；鼓舞，激励

Unit Five

Text

alternative /ɔːl'təːnətiv/	*adj.* 供选择的；选择性的；交替的
beneficial /,beni'fiʃəl/	*adj.* helpful 有益的，有利的；可享利益的
benefit /'benifit/	*n.* 利益，好处；救济金
	vt. 有益于，对……有益 *vi.* 受益，得益
community /kə'mju:niti/	*n.* 社区
crime /kraim/	*n.* 罪行，犯罪；罪恶；犯罪活动
criminal /'kriminəl/	*n.* 罪犯 *adj.* 犯罪的；刑事的；罪恶的
define /di'fain/	*vt.* 定义；使明确；规定

emergency /i'mɜːdʒənsi/	n. 紧急情况　adj. 紧急的；备用的
emergent /i'mɜːdʒənt/	adj. 紧急的
forger /'fɔːdʒə/	n. 铁匠；伪造者
graffiti /grə'fiːti/	n. 墙上乱写乱画的东西（graffito 的复数形式）
innocent /'inəsənt/	adj. 无罪的；无辜的；无知的
jail /dʒeil/	n. prison 监狱；监牢；拘留所　vt. 监禁；下狱
judge /dʒʌdʒ/	vt. 判断；审判　n. 法官　vi. 审判；判决
justice /'dʒʌstis/	n. 司法；正义
litter /'litə/	n. rubbish, garbage 垃圾
offender /ə'fendə/	n. 冒犯者；违法者；罪犯
offense /ə'fens/	n. 犯罪，过错；触怒
scrub /skrʌb/	vt. wipe 用力擦洗
sentence /'sentəns/	n. 宣判，判决；句子，命题　vt. 判决，宣判
shoplifter /'ʃɒpˌliftə/	n. 商店扒手
snatch /snætʃ/	vt. pull violently 夺得
victim /'viktim/	n. 牺牲者；受害人；牺牲品
wrongdoer /'rɒŋˌduːə/	n. people who do wrong 做坏事的人；违法犯罪者
be up to	取决于……
be likely to	有可能……
emergency room	急救室
in jail	坐牢
not do anyone any good	对任何人都没什么好处
to see for himself	(idiom) to see with his own eyes

Reading

absurd /əb'sɜːd/	n. 荒诞；荒诞作品　adj. 荒谬的；可笑的
accountant /ə'kauntənt/	n. 会计师；会计人员
acquisition /ˌækwi'ziʃən/	n. 获得物，获得
activation /ˌækti'veiʃən/	n. 激活；活化作用
additional /ə'diʃənəl/	adj. 附加的，额外的
analytic /ˌænə'litik/	adj. 分析的；解析的；善于分析的

category /'kætigəri/	*n.* 类别；分类
creative /kri'eitiv/	*adj.* 创造性的
creativity /ˌkriei'tiviti/	*n.* 创造力；创造性
diligence /'dilidʒəns/	*n.* 勤奋，勤勉
executor /'eksikjuːtə/	*n.* 执行者；实施者
hemisphere /'hemiˌsfiə/	*n.* 半球
inborn /'inbɔːn/	*adj.* 天生的；先天的
innovation /ˌinəu'veiʃən/	*n.* 创新，革新；新方法
peculiar /pi'kjuːljə/	*n.* 特权；特有财产 *adj.* 特殊的；独特的
peculiarity /piˌkjuːli'æriti/	*n.* 特性；特质；怪癖；奇特
personality /ˌpəːsə'næliti/	*n.* 个性；性格
subscribe /səb'skraib/	*vi.* 订阅；捐款；认购；赞成；签署
undertake /ˌʌndə'teik/	*vt.* 承担，保证；从事；同意；试图
vice versa	反之亦然
zeal /ziːl/	*n.* 热情；热心；热诚

Unit Six

Text

argue /'ɑːgjuː/	*v.* 辩论，争论；证明；说服
banner /'bænə/	*n.* 旗帜，横幅；标语
choice /tʃɔis/	*n.* 选择；选择权；精选品
choose /tʃuːz/	*vt.* 选择，决定
creature /'kriːtʃə/	*n.* 动物，生物；人；创造物
deafening /'defəniŋ/	*adj.* 震耳欲聋的；极喧闹的
defender /di'fendə/	*n.* 防卫者，守卫者
dramatic /drə'mætik/	*adj.* 戏剧的；引人注目的
gasp /gɑːsp, gæsp/	*n.* 喘气 *vt.* 气喘吁吁地说
horn /hɔːn/	*n.* 喇叭
joyous /'dʒɔiəs/	*adj.* 令人高兴的；充满欢乐的
maintain /mein'tein/	*vt.* 维持；继续；维修
miracle /'mirəkl/	*n.* 奇迹，奇迹般的人或物

newsmaker /'njuːzˌmeikə/	n. 制造新闻的事件；新闻人物
octopus /'ɔktəpəs/	n. 章鱼
organise /'ɔːgənaiz/	vt. 组织
overcome /ˌəuvə'kʌm/	v. 战胜，克服
party /'pɑːti/	n. 政党，党派；聚会
referee /ˌrefə'riː/	n. 裁判员；调解人；介绍人
reflect /ri'flek/	v. 反射；表明；考虑
scene /siːn/	n. 场景；现场，景色
security /si'kjuəriti/	n. 安全；保证
slang /slæŋ/	n. 俚语；行话
tournament /'tuənəmənt/	n. 锦标赛，联赛；比赛
triumphant /trai'ʌmfənt/	adj. 成功的；得意洋洋的；狂欢的
trumpet /'trʌmpit/	n. 喇叭；喇叭声
tuneless /'tjuːnlis/	adj. 不和谐的；不成调子的
unfounded /ˌʌn'faundid/	adj. 无理由的；未建立的
volunteer /ˌvɔlən'tiə/	n. 志愿者；志愿兵
as with	正如
be sent off the field	被罚出场外
come out	出现，露面
extra time	【体育】加时赛
go for	攻击；尽力想求得
passing game	传切战术
send off	驱逐离场
Brazil /brə'zil/	巴西（拉丁美洲国家）
Dutch /dʌtʃ/	adj. 荷兰的；荷兰人的；荷兰语的 n. 荷兰人；荷兰语
Howard Webb	（英格兰裁判）霍华德·韦伯
Madrid /mə'drid/	马德里（西班牙首都）
Netherlands /'neðələndz/	荷兰
South Africa	南非
Spain /spein/	西班牙
the World Cup	世界杯

Reading

addiction /ə'dikʃən/	*n.* 上瘾，沉溺；癖嗜	
adjustment /ə'dʒʌstmənt/	*n.* 调整，调节；调节器	
affect /ə'fekt/	*vt.* 影响；假装	
domestic /də'mestik/	*adj.* 国内的；家庭的	
exhausted /ig'zɔːstid/	*adj.* 疲惫的；耗尽的	
insist /in'sist/	*vt.* 坚持，强调 *vi.* 坚持，强调	
monthlong /'mʌnθ'lɔŋ/	*adj.* 整月的	
poll /pəul/	*vt.* 投票；剪短	
pressure /'preʃə(r)/	*n.* 压力；压迫；压强	
relieve /ri'liːv/	*vt.* 解除，减轻	
resident /'rezidənt/	*n.* 居民	
supervisor /ˌsjuːpə'vaizə/	*n.* 监督人，管理人；检查员	
survey /sə:'vei/	*n.* 调查 *vt.* 调查；勘测	
technician /tek'niʃən/	*n.* 技师，技术员；技巧纯熟的人	
urban /'ə:bən/	*adj.* 城市的；住在都市的	
due to	由于；应归于	
kick off	中线开球	
side effect	副作用	
tune in	收听；调谐；使……协调	

(Ⅱ)

A

absurd /əb'sə:d/	*n.* 荒诞；荒诞作品　*adj.* 荒谬的；可笑的
access /'ækses/	*n.* 接近，进入
accessible /ək'sesəbl/	*adj.* 易接近的；可进入的；可理解的
accountant /ə'kauntənt/	*n.* 会计师；会计人员
acquisition /,ækwi'ziʃən/	*n.* 获得物，获得
activation /,ækti'veiʃən/	*n.* 激活；活化作用
addiction /ə'dikʃən/	*n.* 上瘾，沉溺；癖嗜
additional /ə'diʃənəl/	*adj.* 附加的，额外的
address /ə'dres/	*n.* 地址；演讲　*vt.* 演说；从事
adjustment /ə'dʒʌstmənt/	*n.* 调整，调节；调节器
affect /ə'fekt/	*vt.* 影响；假装
agency /'eidʒənsi/	*n.* 代理，中介；代理处，经销处
agent /'eidʒənt/	*n.* 代理人，代理商；药剂；特工
album /'ælbəm/	*n.* 相簿；唱片集；集邮簿；签名纪念册
alter /'ɔ:ltə/	*vt.* 改变，更改
alternative/ɔ:l'tə:nətiv/	*adj.* 供选择的；选择性的；交替的
analytic /,ænə'litik/	*adj.* 分析的；解析的；善于分析的
appeal /ə'pi:l/	*n.* 呼吁，请求；吸引力，感染力　*vt.* 对……上诉
argue /'ɑ:gju:/	*v.* 辩论，争论；证明；说服
assign /ə'sain/	*vt.* 分配；指派；赋值
astonishing /ə'stɔniʃiŋ/	*adj.* 惊人的；令人惊讶的
astronaut /'æstrənɔ:t/	*n.* 宇航员
automatically /,ɔ:tə'mætikəli/	*adv.* 自动地；机械地；无意识地
Avatar	电影《阿凡达》
awful	*adj.* 可怕的，庄严的

B

ballad	*n.* 民歌；情歌；叙事诗歌
banjo /'bændʒəu/	*n.* 班卓琴
banner /'bænə/	*n.* 旗帜，横幅；标语
bar /bɑ:/	*n.* 酒吧；障碍　*vt.* ban 禁止
basically /'beisikəli/	*adv.* mainly 主要地，基本上
be into…	对……很有兴趣，极喜欢；懂得
be up to	取决于……
beneficial /ˌbeni'fiʃəl/	*adj.* helpful 有益的，有利的；可享利益的
benefit /'benifit/	*n.* 利益，好处；救济金
Boise /'bɔisi/	博伊西（美国爱达荷州首府）
bookkeeping /'buk,ki:piŋ/	*n.* 记账，簿记
booklet /'buklit/	*n.* 小册子
Brazil /brə'zil/	巴西（拉丁美洲国家）
bring back	拿回来；使……恢复；使……回忆起来
bureau /'bjuərəu/	*n.* 局，处；衣柜；办公桌

C

calmly /'kɑ:mli/	*adv.* 冷静地；平静地；安静地
category	*n.* 类别；分类
chant /tʃɑ:nt, tʃænt/	*n.* 圣歌；赞美诗
characteristic /ˌkærəktə'ristik/	*n.* 特征；特性；特色
choice /tʃɔis/	*n.* 选择；选择权；精选品
choose /tʃu:z/	*vt.* 选择，决定
chord /kɔ:d/	*n.* 弦；和弦
chorus /'kɔ:rəs/	*n.* 合唱队；齐声　*vt.* 合唱
circle /'sə:kl/	*vt.* 环绕……移动
classical /'klæsikəl/	*n.* 古典音乐　*adj.* 古典的；经典的
client /'klaiənt/	*n.* 顾客，委托人
combat /kəm'bæt/	*vt.* 反对；与……战斗　*vi.* 战斗；搏斗

come out	出现，露面
command module	指挥舱；驾驶舱
commander /kə'mɑːndə/	*n.* 指挥官
community /kə'mjuːniti/	*n.* 社区
contender /kən'tendə/	*n.* 竞争者；争夺者
coordinate /kəu'ɔːdinit; kəu'ɔːdineit/	*n.* 同等的人物 *v.* 协调，整合，综合
creative /kri'eitiv/	*adj.* 创造性的
creativity /ˌkriei'tiviti/	*n.* 创造力；创造性
creature /'kriːtʃə/	*n.* 动物，生物；人；创造物
crew /kruː/	*n.* 队，组；全体人员，全体船员
crime /kraim/	*n.* 罪行，犯罪；罪恶；犯罪活动
criminal /'kriminəl/	*n.* 罪犯 *adj.* 犯罪的；刑事的；罪恶的

D

deafening /'defəniŋ/	*adj.* 震耳欲聋的；极喧闹的
defender /di'fendə/	*n.* 防卫者，守卫者
define /di'fain/	*vt.* 定义；使明确；规定
definitely /'definitli/	*adv.* 清楚地，当然；明确地，肯定地
demo /'deməu/	*n.* 演示；样本唱片
depend on	取决于；依赖于
depth /depθ/	*n.* 深度；深奥
diligence /'dilidʒəns/	*n.* 勤奋，勤勉
disaster /ˌdi'zɑːstə/	*n.* 灾难，灾祸；不幸
domestic /də'mestik/	*adj.* 国内的；家庭的
dominate /'dɔmineit/	*v.* 控制；处于支配地位
down-to-earth /'dauntə'əːθ/	*adj.* 实际的；现实的
dramatic /drə'mætik/	*adj.* 戏剧的；引人注目的
dreamscape /'driːmskeip/	*n.* 梦幻景象，幻景
Dutch /dʌtʃ/	*adj.* 荷兰的；荷兰人的；荷兰语的 *n.* 荷兰人；荷兰语

due to	由于；应归于

E

emergency /i'mə:dʒənsi/	*n.* 紧急情况　*adj.* 紧急的；备用的
emergency room	急救室
emergent /i'mə:dʒənt/	*adj.* 紧急的
enchanting /in'tʃɑ:ntiŋ, en-/	*adj.* 迷人的；妩媚的
end up	结束；死亡
Endeavour /in'devə/	"奋进"号航天飞机
enhance /in'hɑ:ns, -hæns/	*vt.* 提高；加强；增加
entrepreneur /ˌɔntrəprə'nə:/	*n.* 企业家
equipment /i'kwipmənt/	*n. device* 设备，装备；器材
establish /i'stæbliʃ/	*vt.* 建立；创办；安置
even when	即使当
executor /'eksikju:tə/	*n.* 执行者；实施者
exhausted /ig'zɔ:stid/	*adj.* 疲惫的；耗尽的
exist /ig'zist/	*vi.* 存在；生存；生活；继续存在
existence /ig'zistəns/	*n.* 存在；生存；生活；存在物
expansion /ik'spænʃən/	*n.* 膨胀；阐述；扩张物
explode /ik'spləud/	*v.* 爆炸
explosive /ik'spləusiv/	*n.* 炸药；爆炸物　*adj.* 爆炸的；爆炸性的
eyewear /'aiˌwɛə/	*n.* 眼镜；眼镜防护；护目镜

F

favorite /'feivərit/	*adj.* 最喜爱的；中意的；宠爱的
feature /'fi:tʃə/	*n.* 特色，特征　*vt.* 特写；以……为特色
fix /fiks/	*vt.* 使固定；修理；安装
flier /'flaiə/	*n.* 飞行员；飞行物
folk /fəuk/	*n.* 民族；亲属（复数）　*adj.* 民间的
forger /'fɔ:dʒə/	*n.* 铁匠；伪造者

forum /ˈfɔːrəm/	*n.* 论坛，讨论会
freelancer /ˈfriːlɑːnsə(r)/	*n.* 自由记者；自由作家
FTC	*abbr.* （美）联邦贸易委员会（Federal Trade Commission）
fuzzy /ˈfʌzi/	*adj.* 模糊的；失真的；有绒毛的

G

gasp /gɑːsp, gæsp/	*n.* 喘气 *vt.* 气喘吁吁地说
genre /ˈʒɒnrə/	*n.* 流派；体裁；种类
get to	到达；开始；着手处理；接触到
go for	攻击；尽力想求得
go on	继续；过去；继续下去；发生
gospel music	福音音乐（美国黑人的一种宗教音乐）
graffiti /grəˈfiːti/	*n.* 墙上乱写乱画的东西（**graffito** 的复数形式）
grow up	成长，逐渐形成

H

hacker /ˈhækə/	*n.* 电脑黑客
handful /ˈhændful/	*n.* 少数；一把；棘手事
hardship /ˈhɑːdʃip/	*n.* 困苦；苦难；艰难险阻
hater /ˈheitə/	*n.* 怀恨者
heighten	*v.* 提高，升高
hemisphere /ˈhemiˌsfiə/	*n.* 半球
hip hop	嘻哈文化
horn /hɔːn/	*n.* 喇叭
Idaho /ˈaidəhəu/	美国爱达荷州

I

| ignorant /ˈignərənt/ | *adj.* 无知的；愚昧的 |

ignore /igˈnɔː/	*vt.* 驳回诉讼；忽视；不理睬
illusion /iˈljuːʒən/	*n.* 幻觉，错觉；错误的观念或信仰
improvise /ˈimprəvaiz/	*vt.* 即兴创作；即兴表演
in case	万一；假使
in jail	坐牢
inborn /ˈinbɔːn/	*adj.* 天生的；先天的
innocent /ˈinəsənt/	*n.* 天真的人；笨蛋
	adj. 无罪的；无辜的；无知的
innovation /ˌinəuˈveiʃən/	*n.* 创新，革新；新方法
insist /inˈsist/	*vt.* 坚持，强调 *vi.* 坚持，强调
instant /ˈinstənt/	*n.* 瞬间 *adj.* 立即的
instrumentation /ˌinstrumenˈteiʃən/	*n.* 使用仪器；乐器法；仪表化
invoice /ˈinvɔis/	*n.* 发票，单据
issue /ˈiʃjuː, ˈisjuː/	*n.* 问题；发行物 *vt.* 发行，发布
it wouldn't be long before…	不久就……

J

jail /dʒeil/	*n.* prison 监狱；监牢；拘留所 *vt.* 监禁；下狱
joyous /ˈdʒɔiəs/	*adj.* 令人高兴的；充满欢乐的
judge /dʒʌdʒ/	*vt.* 判断；审判 *n.* 法官 *vi.* 审判；判决
justice /ˈdʒʌstis/	*n.* 司法

K

keep up with the Joneses	比阔气；赶时髦（习语）
kick off	中线开球
kid	*n.* 儿童 *v.* 开玩笑

L

lander /ˈlændə/	*n.* 着陆器

laptop /'læptɔp/	*n.* 笔记本电脑
launch /lɔ:ntʃ, lɑ:ntʃ/	*vt. & n.* 发射（导弹、火箭等）；发起
lexicon /'leksikən/	*n.* 词典，辞典
lift off	（火箭等）发射；（直升机）起飞
lightning /'laitniŋ/	*n.* 闪电
link /liŋk/	*n.* 链环，环节；联系，关系
litter /'litə/	*n.* rubbish, garbage 垃圾

M

Madrid /mə'drid/	马德里（西班牙首都）
maintain /mein'tein/	*vt.* 维持；继续；维修
McCall	麦考尔（美国爱达荷州的一个城市）
melody /'melədi/	*n.* 旋律；歌曲；美妙的音乐
miracle /'mirəkl/	*n.* 奇迹，奇迹般的人或物
miss out	错过；遗漏；省略
mission /'miʃən/	*n.* task 使命，任务；delegation 代表团
monthlong /'mʌnθ'lɔŋ/	*adj.* 整月的
motion picture	*n.* 电影
must	*n.* 必须的条件，不可缺少的东西

N

NASA /'næsə, 'nei-/	*abbr.* 美国国家航空航天局（National Aeronautics and Space Administration）
navy /'neivi/	*n.* 海军
Netherlands /'neðələndz/	荷兰
newsmaker /'nju:z,meikə/	*n.* 制造新闻的事件；新闻人物
nonetheless /,nʌnðə'les/	*conj.* 尽管如此，但是

O

octopus /'ɔktəpəs/	*n.* 章鱼
offender /ə'fendə/	*n.* 冒犯者；违法者；罪犯
offense /ə'fens/	*n.* 犯罪，过错；触怒
orbit /'ɔːbit/	*v.* 轨道运行，旋转运动，转圈
orbit /'ɔːbit/	*n.* 轨道；眼眶
organise /'ɔːgənaiz/	*vt.* 组织
origin /'ɔridʒin, 'ɔː-/	*n.* 起源；原点；出身；开端
originate /ə'ridʒəneit/	*v.* 起源，发起；发明
originate /ə'ridʒəneit/	*vt.* 引起；创作 *vi.* 发源；发生；起航
overcome /ˌəuvə'kʌm/	*v.* 战胜，克服
overview /'əuvəvjuː/	*n.* 综述；概观

P

party /'pɑːti/	*n.* 政党，党派；聚会
path /pɑːθ, pæθ/	*n.* 小路；轨道
peculiar /pi'kjuːljə/	*n.* 特权；特有财产 *adj.* 特殊的；独特的
peculiarity /piˌkjuːli'æriti/	*n.* 特性；特质；怪癖；奇特
performer /pə'fɔːmə/	*n.* 执行者；演奏者
personality /ˌpəːsə'næləti/	*n.* 个性；品格；名人
pick up	捡起；获得；收拾
pilot /'pailət/	行员；领航员
poll /pəul/	*v.* 投票；剪短
popular /'pɔpjulə/	*adj.* 流行的，通俗的；受欢迎的
portable /'pɔːtəbl, 'pəu-/	*adj.* 手提的，便携式的；轻便的
premise /'premis/	*n.* 前提；上述各项
pressure /'preʃə(r)/	*n.* 压力；压迫；压强
previous /'priːvjəs/	*adj.* 以前的；早先的；过早的
primarily /'praimərəli, prai'me-/	*adv.* mainly 主要地；首先；根本上
primary /'praiməri/	*adj.* 主要的，首要的

projection /prəu'dʒekʃən/	n. 投射；规划；突出

R

rank among	跻身于；属于之列
rap /ræp/	vt. 抢走；轻敲 vi. 敲击；交谈 n. 说唱乐
rapper /'ræpə/	n. 说唱歌手
rebel /'rebəl, ri'bel/	n. 反叛者；叛徒
referee /ˌrefə'riː/	n. 裁判员；调解人；介绍人
reflect /ri'flekt/	v. 反射；表明；考虑
region /'riːdʒən/	n. 地区；地域；领域
relate with	使相关，使符合
relieve /ri'liːv/	vt. 解除，减轻
remain in	待在屋里，不外出；保持处于（某种状态）
represent /ˌrepri'zent/	vt. 代表；表现；描绘 vi. 代表；提出异议
rescue /'reskjuː/	vt. 援救，救出，营救
resident /'rezidənt/	n. 居民
resurgence /ri'səːdʒəns/	n. 复活；再现；再起
rhyming /'raimiŋ/	n. 押韵 adj. 押韵的
ride /raid/	vt. 骑；乘；控制

S

scene /siːn/	n. 场景；现场，景色
scientific /saiən'tifik/	adj. 科学的
scientific instrument	科学仪器
scratch /skrætʃ/	n. 抓痕，抓的声音，乱写 v. 搔痒，抓，抹掉
scratching their heads	绞尽脑汁
scrub /skrʌb/	vt. wipe 用力擦洗
security /si'kjuəriti/	n. 安全；保证
sensitive /'sensitiv/	adj. 敏感的；灵敏的；易受伤害的
send off	驱逐离场

sentence	*n.* 宣判，判决；句子，命题 *vt.* 判决，宣判
sentiment /'sentimənt/	*n.* 感情，情绪；情操；观点；多愁善感
shoplifter /'ʃɔp,liftə/	*n.* 商店扒手
side effect	副作用
slang /slæŋ/	*n.* 俚语；行话
smug /smʌg/	*n.* 书呆子；自命不凡的家伙
snatch /snætʃ/	*vt.* pull violently 夺得
space shuttle	航天飞机
space station	空间站，太空站
spacecraft /'speiskrɑ:ft, -kræft/	*n.* 宇宙飞船，航天器
Spain /spein/	西班牙
staff /stɑ:f, stæf/	*n.* 职员；参谋
star /stɑ:/	*n.* 星，明星 *vt.* 由……主演 *vi.* 担任主角
stay connected with	保持联系
stimulate /'stimjuleit/	*v.* 刺激；鼓舞，激励
stir /stə:/	*n.* 搅拌；轰动 *vt.* 搅拌；激起；惹起
stirring /'stə:riŋ/	*adj.* 激动人心的；活跃的
subscribe /səb'skraib/	*vi.* 订阅；捐款；认购；赞成；签署
substitute /'sʌbstitju:t, -tu:t/	*n.* 代替者，替代品 *v.* 用……代替，代替……
supervisor /,sju:pə'vaizə/	*n.* 监督人，管理人；检查员
supply /sə'plai/	*n.* 物资；供应品；贮备量
survey /sə:'vei/	*n.* 调查 *vt.* 调查；勘测

T

tailor /'teilə/	*v.* 裁制；调整使适应
technician /tek'niʃən/	*n.* 技师，技术员；技巧纯熟的人
technique /tek'ni:k/	*n.* 技巧，技术；手法
teenager /'ti:neidʒə/	*n.* 十几岁的青少年
tempest /'tempist/	*n.* 大风暴，暴风雨；骚动，风波
tempo /'tempəu/	*n.* 速度，发展速度；拍子
texture /'tekstʃə/	*n.* 质地；纹理；结构；本质，实质

theme /θiːm/	*n.* 主题；主旋律；题目
themed /θiːmd/	*adj.* 以……为主题的
to see for himself	*(idiom)* to see with his own eyes
tournament /ˈtuənəmənt/	*n.* 锦标赛，联赛；比赛
transform /trænsˈfɔːm/	*vt.* 改变，使……变形；转换
triumphant /traiˈʌmfənt/	*adj.* 成功的；得意洋洋的；狂欢的
trumpet /ˈtrʌmpit/	*n.* 喇叭；喇叭声
tune in	收听；调谐；使……协调
tuneless /ˈtjuːnlis/	*adj.* 不和谐的；不成调子的

u

underlying /ˌʌndəˈlaiiŋ/	*adj.* 潜在的；根本的；在下面的；优先的
undertake /ˌʌndəˈteik/	*vt.* 承担，保证；从事；同意；试图
unfounded /ˈʌnˈfaundid/	*adj.* 无理由的；未建立的
unmanned spacecraft	无人驾驶飞机；无人宇宙飞船
urban /ˈəːbən/	*adj.* 城市的；住在都市的
utilize /ˈjuːtilaiz/	*vt.* 利用

v

variation /ˌvɛəriˈeiʃən/	*n.* 变奏曲，变更；变种
venue /ˈvenjuː/	*n.* 场地，场馆
victim /ˈviktim/	*n.* 牺牲者；受害人；牺牲品
video /ˈvidiəu/	*n.* 视频 *adj.* 视频的；录像的；电视的
virtual /ˈvəːtʃuəl/	*adj.* 实质上的，事实上的；虚拟的
vocal harmony	人声合唱
volunteer /ˌvɔlənˈtiə/	*n.* 志愿者；志愿兵
vulgar /ˈvʌlgə/	*adj.* 粗俗的；通俗的；本土的

W

| weird /wɪəd/ | *adj.* 怪异的；不可思议的；超自然的 |
| wrongdoer /'rɒŋ'duːə, 'rɔːŋ-/ | *n.* 做坏事的人；违法犯罪者 |

Y

| youngster /'jʌŋstə/ | *n.* 年轻人；少年 |

Z

| zeal /ziːl/ | *n.* 热情；热心；热诚 |

（Ⅲ）

A

appeal to	*v.* 呼吁；上诉；对……有吸引力
as with	正如

B

be into...	对……很有兴趣，极喜欢；懂得，取决于……
be likely to	有可能……
be sent off the field	被罚出场外
be up to	取决于，该由……负责
bring back	拿回来；使……恢复；使……回忆起来

C

come out	出现，露面
command module	指挥舱；驾驶舱

D

depend on	取决于；依赖于
due to	由于；应归于

E

emergency room	急救室
end up	结束；死亡
even when	即使当
extra time	【体育】加时赛

G

get to	到达；开始；着手处理；接触到
go for	攻击；尽力想求得
go on	继续；过去；继续下去；发生
gospel music	福音音乐（美国黑人的一种宗教音乐）
grow up	成长，逐渐形成

H

hip hop	嘻哈文化
Howard Webb	（英格兰裁判）霍华德·韦伯

I

in case	万一；假使
in jail	坐牢
it wouldn't be long before…	不久就……

K

keep up with the Joneses	比阔气；赶时髦（习语）
kick off	中线开球

L

lift off	（火箭等）发射；（直升机）起飞

M

miss out	错过；遗漏；省略
motion picture	电影

N

| not do anyone any good | 对任何人都没什么好处 |

O

| on earth | 究竟 |

P

passing game	传切战术
pick up	获得
pick up	捡起；获得；收拾

R

rank among	跻身于；属于之列
relate with	使相关，使符合
remain in	待在屋里，不外出；保持处于（某种状态）

S

scientific instrument	科学仪器
scratching their heads	绞尽脑汁
send off	驱逐离场
side effect	副作用
South Africa	南非
space shuttle	航天飞机
space station	空间站，太空站
stay connected with	保持联系

T

the World Cup	世界杯
to see for himself	(*idiom*) to see with his own eyes
tune in	收听；调谐；使……协调

U

| unmanned spacecraft | 无人驾驶飞机；无人宇宙飞船 |

V

| vice versa | 反之亦然 |
| vocal harmony | 人声合唱 |

图书在版编目（CIP）数据

创新思维英语综合教程. 第3册 / 赵培，王雪梅主编. —北京：中国人民大学出版社，2011.4

ISBN 978-7-300-13470-3

Ⅰ.①创… Ⅱ.①赵… ②王… Ⅲ.①英语–高等职业教育–教材 Ⅳ.①H31

中国版本图书馆 CIP 数据核字（2011）第 036819 号

创新思维英语综合教程（第三册）
主 编 赵 培 王雪梅
副主编 袁俊娥 王成霞 邢桂丽
编 委 孙丰田 徐亮璎彧 赵燕婷
Chuangxin Siwei Yingyu Zonghe Jiaocheng (Di-san Ce)

出版发行	中国人民大学出版社	
社 址	北京中关村大街31号	**邮政编码** 100080
电 话	010—62511242（总编室）	010—62511398（质管部）
	010—82501766（邮购部）	010—62514148（门市部）
	010—62515195（发行公司）	010—62515275（盗版举报）
网 址	http://www.crup.com.cn	
	http://www.ttrnet.com（人大教研网）	
经 销	新华书店	
印 刷	北京市易丰印刷有限责任公司	
规 格	170 mm×228 mm 16 开本	**版 次** 2011 年 6 月第 1 版
印 张	13.5	**印 次** 2011 年 6 月第 1 次印刷
字 数	235 000	**定 价** 35.00 元（附赠光盘）